REMO WAS AT THE TOP OF THE STAIRS NOW . . .

But he saw only a flash of saffron robe moving across the stage. Nilsson's arms were extended in front of him, reaching for the girl.

The Viking roar rose again in Nilsson's throat, then died in a curdled squeak as an iron-hard fist came from behind him. He recognized the crunch of his own bones breaking and the slow, lazy feeling of warmth as death overtook his body. He turned toward Chiun, searching those hazel eyes for meaning, but there was only respect.

Down below, the cordon of protection between the bandstand and the audience disappeared. It was a girl who made the first charge. The music slowed and stopped. The sudden silence was like an invitation. Baying like a pack of hounds, the entire audience seemed to surge forward toward the bandstand . . .

The Destroyer #13

WARREN MURPHY & RICHARD SAPIR

ACID ROCK

PINNACLE BOOKS
WINDSOR PUBLISHING CORP.

PINNACLE BOOKS

are published by

Windsor Publishing Corp.
475 Park Avenue South
New York, NY 10016

Fifth printing: February, 1989

Printed in the United States of America

For Alyce, Gary, Vikie, Maureen, Blanche, and Leanora. But most of all for the awesomely magnificent House of Sinanju, P.O. Box 1149, Pittsfield, Massachusetts.

CHAPTER ONE

The day before his flailing body met the Denver sidewalk, accelerating at thirty-two feet per second per second, William Blake lost his temper at the Los Angeles headquarters of the Federal Bureau of Investigation.

It was not that his district supervisor had once again given him an assignment that might keep him away from home for weeks. It was not that Special Agent Blake had to cancel his family's vacation for the second year in a row. It was that the supervisor was so . . . so . . . well, supervisory.

"Damn it, what is Washington worried about?" asked Blake, referring to the place from whence all policy flowed. "I've successfully handled situations like this seven times. At this, I'm probably the best in the whole bureau."

"That's why you're in charge," said District Supervisor Watkins.

"Yeah. I'm in charge, but you're going over where we're going to keep her, who's going to be on duty with her at night, what's she going to eat, and who's going to prepare it."

"I'm just going over the details with you. Two heads are better than one."

"Not if the other one's yours."

"I'll forget you said that, Blake."

"I want you to remember it. I want you to put it in your report. I want you to put down that you're giving advice to the man Washington calls in on all protective custody situations. I want you to tell them that."

Blake straightened his tie. He could feel the heat rising in his neck. Perhaps it was just the summer queasies getting to him, queasies he had hoped to cure with a two-week camping trip. Perhaps. But why was Washington making such a fuss over a simple protective custody? There was a girl, nineteen. The girl was the daughter of a wealthy commodities dealer. She hated her father and was going to testify about some hanky panky with a large Russian grain deal. So what? The biggest problem they faced was that she would change her mind, not that someone was going to kill her.

"Bill, I think you should know. This girl is the target of the largest open contract in history." Watkins's voice was hushed.

"What?" asked Blake, his clear blue eyes widening, his brow wrinkling.

"She is the target of the largest open contract in history, we believe."

"I thought you said that," said Blake. "Open contract, you said."

"The largest open . . ."

"I heard that. I heard that. I heard that." Blake's smooth fortyish face showed sudden wrinkles as he gave way to laughter. "An open contract." He shook his head and laughed some more. "Since J. Edgar, nothing has worked right. What's the matter with you? You should know better."

"This one's for real, Bill."

"Real, unreal, a thousand dollars, a hundred thousand dollars. It's an open contract. Give her a plane ticket, a new name and the date she's supposed to show up to testify and let me go on my vacation."

"We have reason to believe this open contract is for one million dollars. One million dollars."

"Why not ten million? Why not a hundred million?"

"Don't be facetious, Blake."

"I'm not. An open contract is about as dangerous as a head cold. It's a myth invented by newspapermen. When have you ever heard of an open contract being filled? Who's going to fill it?"

"This one, I was told on highest authority, is for real and there are people trying to fill it right now."

"Mr. Watkins, sir. The definition of an open contract is that anyone can make the hit and collect from the man offering the money. But there's a little flaw in that. No one is going to commit murder on the possibility that someone he has never met is going to keep a promise of payment for the murder. Killers don't go knocking people off unless they at least meet the person who wants the job done. I mean, what are they going to do if they don't get paid? Bring the victim back to life? An open contract, sir, to be specific—and hopefully final—does not exist."

"I believe Willie Moretti in New Jersey was killed on an open contract."

"No, sir. If you remember, it was a standing order from all five Mafia families in the New York City area. Now, Joe Valachi was an open contract. He outlived Genovese, who was supposed to have issued it, for $100,000, I believe. Genovese should have made it for a million. It wouldn't have mattered."

Supervisor Watkins looked at Agent Blake and

then back to the file in front of him. In that file was an order, and whether he felt the same way Blake did, did not matter. Blake was to be put in charge and given maximum staffing and other support. One Vickie Stoner, nineteen, female Caucasian, was to reach the Senate hearings on grain fraud, scheduled for two weeks away. And she was to reach them alive.

"Would you feel better, Blake, if I told you it was a closed contract?"

"Yes. Then I would know I am defending against a real opponent."

"Then treat your charge that way."

"In other words, make believe."

"If that will enable you to do a more effective job, yes."

"This could never happen under J. Edgar," said Blake. "We're protecting someone who's supposed to be killed on credit."

Supervisor Watkins ignored this remark. Later he ignored Blake's stated reason for wanting a fifth night man to be assigned. In addition to the ones outside the room, on the roof, in the stairwell and in the hotel lobby, this one was to be placed at the airport.

"Why the airport?" asked Watkins.

"To protect her against low-flying night fairies, sir," said Blake, containing a smile.

"Four men," said Watkins.

"Very good, sir," said Blake.

Watkins also ignored the suggestion about food.

"And we'll make sure no diet soda is used."

"Why is that?" asked the now-suspicious Watkins.

"Cyclamates, sir. It's been proven that if a per-

10

son drinks fifty-five gallons of cyclamates an hour, that person might develop cancer."

"We'll vary the restaurants, as per usual procedure," said Watkins.

"Very good, sir," said Blake.

Miss Stoner was now in L.A. headquarters, said Watkins. Would Blake like to see her now?

"I'd like to tell my son, daughter, and wife first that we're not going to Washington State Park. Then I'll take over, if it's all right with you."

Watkins agreed; it would prove to be Blake's first mistake. He said he would be back in two hours and put the assignment out of his thoughts.

He drove to his small ranch house with the neat lawn and the bicycle sprawled in the driveway. He did not scold his son for the driveway obstruction. He called him into the den.

"I'd like to explain about the bicycle, Pop. I was out on the lawn with Jimmy Tolliver and the ice cream truck . . ."

"That's all right," Blake told his son.

"Something wrong, Pop?"

"Yes, in a way. You know that camping trip we were going to take? Well, we'll have to postpone it this year."

Blake was surprised to see his son just shrug.

"I'm sorry," Blake said.

"That's okay, Pop. I really wasn't looking forward to all those bugs at night. Maybe we can go to Disneyland sometime, okay?"

"But we always go to Disneyland. We've been there twice this year already."

"Yeah, but I like Disneyland."

"I thought you had your heart set on Washington State Park."

"That was you, Pop. I never wanted to go that much."

Neither had his daughter, Blake found out, and this relieved some of the burden of telling his wife.

"What is it this time, Bill?" she said, setting the table and avoiding his eyes.

"I can't say. I'll be out of town for a while. Maybe two weeks."

"I see," she said coldly.

"I'm sorry."

"You were sorry last year, you'll be sorry next year. I guess it's the way with the bureau, isn't it? To be sorry? We're having squash tonight. You like squash."

"If I had a choice, you know I wouldn't disappoint you again."

"Does it matter? Get washed up. We'll be eating in a minute."

"I can't stay."

Mrs. Blake scooped up one place setting and ran into the kitchen. Blake followed his wife. She was crying.

"Go. Just go," she sobbed. "I know you have to go. So just go."

"I love you," he said.

"What difference does that make? Just get out of here."

He tried to kiss her but she twisted her head away. She would remember, for the rest of her life, denying him that last kiss.

When Blake returned to headquarters, he realized his mistake. Two agents were in a side office talking.

"It's in there," said one, lifting his eyes to the ceiling. "We've got a real winner this time."

"How long has she been in there? Did she eat supper?"

"She says she doesn't have to eat. Eating is selfish."

"You check on her?"

"An hour ago. She says she doesn't know why she should be kept in prison when she hasn't done anything wrong. If you ask me, I'd like to see even more space in the generation gap."

"You should be with her," said Blake, and entered the room without a backward glance. It was dark. Blake turned on the lights.

"Damn," he said.

Flowing red hair cascaded over the arm of a chair. Two young white legs poked crazily over its back. The chest did not move. No apparent breathing. The loose tie-dyed tee shirt was motionless.

Blake rushed to the still form and put his ear to the heart. Was that a beat? Yes. Strong. Beating strongly.

"Let's ball," said the faint voice and Blake felt the voice vibrations against his cheek. He stood up. Her crystal blue eyes had pupils the size of pinheads. The light pink lips formed a weak, silly grin.

"Let's ball," she said.

"Miss Stoner, what did you take?"

"A trip to the mountain. I'm on the mountain. The mountain. Fuhhh-reaked out. Fuhhh-reaked."

"Did Miss Stoner have a pocketbook, bag, anything?" Blake called to the other agents.

"Yeah, Bill. Sort of a small pouch."

"Search it and give me the drugs."

Blake watched the girl try to focus her eyes.

"No drugs here," said the other agent.

13

"I'm going to search her. Get in here," said Blake, who wanted a witness and corroborating testimony should the girl later claim an improper advance was made against her.

Her blue jeans were faded and tight. Blake patted the pockets and felt a small vial.

As he reached for it, she said:

"Foreplay. Good. I like foreplay."

The pills were like small yellow aspirin tablets.

"Mescaline?" asked Blake.

"No thanks, I'm already turned on," said Vickie Stoner.

"She's all yours," said the agent.

"She's ours," corrected Blake. "I want two men with her at all times. At all times." Blake checked his watch. They would miss the evening flight to Washington, D.C. He wasn't going to take her on a plane in this condition. Blake and the two agents sat with her during the night. Just before dawn, she began to cry, then she closed her eyes and went to sleep. When she awoke, she was ravenous. She wanted three super-burgers, a double order of french fries, a cola and a milkshake.

They drove to a drive-in hamburger stand and when they left, she demanded they stop at a cigar store. She said she wanted a chocolate bar and just couldn't go on without one. Blake thought she was too long inside the store and started in after her, but he met her in the doorway. "Just something I had to do," she explained, but would not tell him what it was. He noticed she did not have a chocolate bar in her hand.

As they neared the airport, she turned on the radio and kept moving the dial until what appeared to be static with a beat came from the speakers. The words bespoke a strong dissatisfaction with the world and a need for someone, which Blake assumed to be sexual.

Vickie Stoner nodded her head to the music and when the news came on, she shut her eyes.

The lead story was about last night's flight from Los Angeles to Washington. It had crashed over the Rockies. Witnesses reported what appeared to be an explosion in the tail assembly. One hundred persons were killed.

Blake signaled the car ahead to pull over. The one behind also pulled over.

Ten men in suits, ties, and shined cordovans gathered at the side of the road. They all wore snap-brim hats.

"All right. You, you, you and you," said Blake. "Get into lounging clothes. I don't want to see any two men in standard dress. You and you, don't shave for a while. You and you, get the parts out of your hair. That crewcut we can't do anything with, so you keep your hat on."

"What's up, Bill?"

"Our flight to Washington was bombed last night. I don't know if it has anything to do with us, but we were supposed to be on that plane when it blew up over the Rockies. We were told that Miss Stoner's life is in danger. I guess we should act accordingly. This is what we're going to do. We're not flying to Washington. We're going to assume there are real killers after Miss Stoner's life. That means an attack could come from anywhere. So we're going to be careful. We're driving to Denver, but not in three look-alike government pool cars. You and you, rent the jazziest car you can get. You and you, get a truck. You and you, get a heavy four-door car, maybe a Cadillac or Lincoln."

"Rent?"

15

"Unless you own one."

"We'll rent."

"Okay. You, get back to Watkins. Tell him we're driving to Denver. We're going to get rooms in the hotel that faces the Rockies, so we don't have to worry about anyone sniping from a window across the street. We'll check in with Supervisor Watkins when we get there."

"If we use rented cars, we won't have radio contact," one agent noted.

"I'll sacrifice that for not being noticed," Blake said.

"Sir, do you really think there is an open contract out on Miss Stoner's life? I mean, one that is being picked up?"

"I think we were lucky we didn't take that flight last night is what I think. I think we're going to stay lucky. There's a luncheonette with a parking lot just outside of Watts. Brubaw's. Everyone know where it is?"

There were some assents and a few nos. Blake paired the ones who knew with those who didn't and returned to his government car.

"Okeydokey," said Blake, smiling.

"What does that mean?" asked Vickie Stoner. "Okeydokey?"

"It means we're in good shape, Miss Stoner."

"Heavy, man," said Vickie.

At the hotel in Denver, Blake organized his men in a diamond pattern that he found out, late in life, was also used by the Viet Cong when they camped. He had learned it from an old hand who said his father had learned it from a Texas ranger.

One man was posted on a street north of the hotel, another was posted south. Close to the room, east and west on the street directly below, were other men. That was the outer perimeter.

The rooms above and to the sides of Miss Stoner's were also rented by Blake's agents. And one man floated within the diamond, checking the points without being obvious.

Blake and two other agents shared the suite with Vickie Stoner, who appeared bored with television and wanted records of Maggot and the Dead Meat Lice.

"Someday, I'm gonna ball that Maggot," said Vickie, pointing to an album cover of what appeared to Blake to be a derelict with blue paint under his eyes and three lamp chops hanging from the chest of his white satin jumpsuit. "He's the baddest," Vickie said.

"That's negative?" asked Blake.

"That's positive," said Vickie.

"Do you want to see something very baddest?" asked Blake.

Vickie smiled at his use of language. "Sure," she said.

Blake did not bother to strap on his gun, because then, to eliminate any chance of drawing attention to himself, he would have had to put on his jacket, and they were only going out on the balcony.

He opened the glass doors and there it was, deep in the west, the sun setting behind the Rockies.

"Yeah, heavy," said Vickie. "Heavy."

"Those are the Rockies, the most beautiful mountains in the world, but also some of the most treacherous."

"Like life, too, you know," said Vickie. "If it's heavy, it can also be a bummer, know what I mean?"

"Yes," said Blake. "It smells better over there, too. No air pollution."

17

"Wait a few years, man, you won't be able to breathe there either."

Blake smiled. "A bit pessimistic, aren't you?"

"What I see is what we got."

"Is that why you're going to testify?"

"That, and other things. I don't think the pigs should have things their way all the time. My father's got enough money. It's not right to rip off wheat from this country and drive up the price of poor people's bread."

"Am I a pig?" Blake asked.

Vickie giggled. "No. You're heavy. Straight as shit, but heavy, man. Like candy."

"You're not baddest at all," said Blake, and saw her giggle into her hands like young girls did back in Kansas City when he was going to high school and the big daring high was wine and good girls didn't do it unless they were married. It was a changing country, but how bad could it be, how bad could this counter-culture be, if a girl like Vickie was willing to testify against her father just because she thought something was wrong? Wasn't that what they had taught us?

"Don't they ever stop working?" asked Vickie, pointing to the roof and to the right.

Blake looked up. A painter's scaffold, its white slatted bottom coming toward them was descending from the roof. Blake could see shoes and bodies through the gaps between the slats, like black blobs against the darkening sky.

The platform lowered silently and that, more than the odd hour, told Blake they were definitely under attack. Scaffolds always squeaked, even when new. The pulleys would have to be muffled with packed grease to insure silence, and no painter, sand blaster, or steam sprayer would risk a slip just for quiet. Only a killer would.

18

"Vickie, go inside and tell one of the agents to bring me my shoulder holster, would you please?" said Blake in a very casual voice.

"You going to target shoot twelve stories down?"

"No. Just do as I say, will you, honey?"

"Okeydokey," said Vickie, using her new word. The scaffold was descending just to the right of the balcony. If Blake had brought the radio gear he could have gotten the upstairs room to move on it first. But the radio gear and the government cars were back in Los Angeles. And that was the flaw in the diamond defense. The points weren't connected.

From behind Blake came a knock on the hotel suite door.

"Room service."

"Don't answer it," yelled Blake and with his shout, the scaffold came down quickly and he heard the door to the room open and Vickie scream. One agent was caught with a blast in the belly, but the other returned fire. In the room, the two side doors opened and there was more firing, and just above his head Blake saw a rifle poke down from the scaffold. He yanked and pulled a blond young man along with the rifle. With a snap of his elbow into the man's jaw, he knocked him into the bannister. The rifle disappeared over the railing. Three other men were coming down on the scaffold and Blake was weaponless. He grabbed one of the ropes, braced his feet against the railing, and pushed. One man fell; the remaining two were unable to fire.

Blake pushed again with his body, like a maniac working a playground swing. The scaffold swung far out from the side of the hotel wall. He felt a banging on his back, but he swung back to the

19

wall again and pushed with his legs. Then the heavily greased pulley slipped and his end of the scaffold plunged down. He might have held on with his hands if he hadn't gotten a face and chest full of two sliding men. His hands popped free like two weak safety pins attached to a bail of hay.

Blake hit the Denver sidewalk accelerating, as would any other free-falling object, at thirty-two feet per second per second. The sidewalk remained stationary. They met. Blake felt a crack, and then nothing. He would never feel again.

The last man who fell from the scaffold hit his companion and his fall was cushioned just enough for him to live a day. Before he died of multiple injuries, he told FBI men about an open contract he was trying to fill. The whole gang were beach bums; they had thought that eight of them could pull it off. It was sort of a lark, but if it had worked, they would have been rich for life.

The killing had been a holocaust. Four agents dead. Eight assailants dead. Not in this century had that many people been killed in a federal shoot-out.

But there were indications that even worse might be around the corner. At the funerals of the young men, a single large wreath was delivered for each one. A bright gold envelope with silver lettering was attached. Each envelope had a tassel on it.

When the tassels were pulled, each envelope spilled forth $12,500 in twenty-dollar bills and a note made of letters cut from magazines and pasted on a sheet, almost like a kidnapper's ransom note.

The note read:

"For services almost rendered."

20

Someone had been willing to pay $100,000 just for an unsuccessful try. The open contract was real.

The wreaths were confiscated as evidence. When the families of two of the dead men wanted to know why, they were told only that the wreaths might lead to the men who had hired the deceased. The funeral directors were warned about the dangers of disclosing the contents of the envelopes to anyone. Word was leaked to the press that the shoot-out was over a narcotics shipment. But the most emphasis was placed on keeping mum about the cash. There was trouble enough without helping to advertise an open contract.

During the shooting at the Denver hotel, Vickie Stoner had disappeared. She might still be alive somewhere. Supervisor Watkins confided to a special agent that he thought the situation was hopeless, that the girl was as good as dead. Later, when he tried to call the same special agent back to mention one other fact, he was told that no such agent existed.

"But you okayed him," complained Watkins.

"We did not," said the director's aide at headquarters.

In Washington, D. C., the man who had posed as a special agent finished writing his report, which he thought was for the National Security Agency. He had done many reports like it. On the two Kennedy assassinations, on the King killing and on many other, discreet deaths that had not made headlines. Officially, he was the authority on specific personnel functions, which translated into assassination. He gauged the professional quality of these happenings and determined their likely points of origin. An assassination was like a fingerprint. It could tell you which nation or

21

which group was responsible. Each nation had a man like this.

His report concluded that the attempt on the life of Vickie Stoner had obviously been planned by someone with a lot of intelligence and very little experience—which ruled out any foreign power. It was his belief that the men who had attempted the assassination were also the planners of it. Certainly there was nothing in the attempt to suggest that it was beyond the capability of beach bums.

What was of special interest, his report stated, was that this was an open contract, something he had read about but had assumed did not exist, for reasons obvious to anyone familiar with the field. This open contract was real and payable, and the money in the funeral wreaths was proof.

It was inevitable that experienced professionals would now attempt to collect the sum, if Vickie Stoner was still alive—which was doubtful. Supervisor Watkins had stated the case accurately: "hopeless." But it was of no concern to N.S.A., since no foreign power was involved.

So ended his summary, and the directors of the N.S.A. did not even bother to completely read it. "No foreign power" put it out of their jurisdiction. As a matter of fact, they had not even ordered the report. A secondary-level official had. He had sent a Xerox of it along to his superior, who he assumed was engaged in some kind of watchdog agency.

Twelve hours had passed between the time Supervisor Watkins had said "hopeless" and the time the Xerox copy of the report landed on a desk in Folcraft Sanitarium in Rye, New York.

At Folcraft the report was read thoroughly; it was there that the order for it had originated. A lemon-faced man scanned the words, jotted some semireadable notes to himself and then filed the copy in a round tube, which shredded it.

He leaned back in his chair and looked out through the one-way glass toward the Long Island Sound, dark now, waiting for the sun.

Hopeless? Maybe not. An interesting equation was at work here. If Miss Stoner were alive, then more competent assassins would go after her. And if *they* were stopped, then only more competent ones would come. An acceleration of excellence, leading to the very best wherever or whoever he or they might be.

Dr. Harold Smith looked out into the darkness. Wherever they might be. He knew where they were. He was going to send them a telegram. But Vickie Stoner would not worry. The best in the world would be on her side; she need only worry about the second best.

Dr. Smith dialed Western Union himself. His secretary had long since gone home. He gave the name of the person he wished the telegram sent to, and then the message:

"Aunt Mildred to visit tomorrow. She wants the green room."

CHAPTER TWO

His name was Remo and he didn't care when Aunt Mildred was arriving or what room she wanted, and why didn't Western Union go back to the singing telegram, he wondered aloud.

Instead of returning the receiver to the cradle,

he placed thumb and forefinger over the telephone cord and with a gentle snap yanked it out of the wall. It was 4:30 A.M.

His suite in Atlanta's Hyatt Regency was air conditioned to a just bearable chill, only slightly more pleasant than the oppressive heat that was building up for the coming day. His mouth tasted of salt, but Chiun had said it would taste of salt. He went to the bathroom and let the water run and when it was cold stuck his mouth to the faucet and filled it.

Sloshing the water around his mouth, he went to the darkened living room of the hotel suite. On a bare portion of the floor slept a frail figure on a mat, a black kimono reaching from the toes to the wisps of white hair. Chiun, the latest Master of Sinanju.

One did not wake the Master of Sinanju, especially not his pupil, even though Remo was never quite sure when Chiun was asleep or in one of his fifty-nine stages of relaxation, sleep being the fifty-second. Someday, Chiun had said, Remo would achieve these same stages, even though he had started his enlightenment late and even though he was only a white man.

Why was Remo so lucky that he would learn all those stages, Remo had wondered. Because the Master of Sinanju could do wonders with nothing, the nothing being Remo.

"Thanks for your confidence, Little Father," Remo had said and then Chiun had warned him of the coming night of the salt. On that night, Chiun had said, Remo would doubt himself and his abilities and would do something foolish to prove to himself that his skills and training were valid. "But in your case, there will be a problem."

"What problem, Little Father?"

24

"How will you be able to tell when you do something foolish, since it is so much like everything else you do," Chiun had said, and thought that this was amazingly funny, so funny he repeated it for days and attributed the fact that Remo did not appreciate the witticism to Remo's typical white man's lack of humor.

Sinanju was a village in North Korea, whose poor and young were supported by the labors of the Master of Sinanju, plying the trade of the professional assassin. Chiun, even though eighty years old, was the reigning master of Sinanju. He had himself experienced the night of the salt when he was twelve years old, almost as a rite of puberty. It was another sign of the body becoming something else, he explained.

"What else?" Remo asked.

But Chiun did not answer his pupil, for as he pointed out, a man who lacked a sense of humor also surely lacked wisdom.

"But you don't think it's funny when someone mistakes you for Chinese or Japanese, instead of Korean."

"He who does not distinguish between insult and witticism certainly cannot understand the deeper meanings of Sinanju."

"Why is it that when you insult me, it's humor, but when someone passes a harmless remark about you, it's an insult?" Remo asked.

"Perhaps you will never achieve the night of the salt," Chiun had said.

But Remo had and here it was, and although his mouth was still filled with water, he tasted the salt as if someone had emptied a shaker of it into his mouth. Remo went back to the bathroom and spat out the water. He was in his thirties and for more than a decade he had been

25

changing, first his mind, and then his very nervous system.

So he had become what Chiun had said he would become. An assassin was not something one did, but something one was. From time to time, of course, Chiun had warned, Remo's early improper training would crop up like poisons in the blood becoming boils on the skin. But with each boil his body would be cleansed.

"Of things like decency, right?" Remo had said.

But why should Remo care? He was a dead man anyhow, according to his fingerprints, which had been retired the night he was electrocuted for a murder he didn't commit. Of course, the electrocution hadn't quite worked and Remo had found himself pressed into service as the super-secret killer arm of a super-secret government agency, empowered by the President to fight crime outside the law. The whole thing had been supposed to take only a few years, and now Remo was in his thirties and he had neither home, nor family, nor even last name, and there was salt in his mouth. The first white man ever to achieve that stage. Remo gulped another mouthful of water from the still running faucet and sloshed it around. To hell with it. He was going outside.

He spat the water into the bathroom light switch, hoping to cause an electrical short circuit to see if he could really create the sort of pressure Chiun had talked about. All he got was a wet light switch. He left the door open under the assumption that if a team of burglars should wander in and attack the eighty-year-old Chiun in his sleep, it was their fault and they had it coming.

The revitalized Downtown Atlanta was suspiciously like the old unrevitalized Downtown Atlanta. Heavy oppressive air and a general feeling of discomfort. Remo walked to the bus station. Bus stations in every town across America were always open.

Why was it people at bus stations at this hour always appeared to be without hope? Remo bought a newspaper. The Atlanta Eagles had begun summer training and the rookies were reporting. *This* year, according to the coach, their rookie crop was the best and they had a good shot at the National Football League title, even though their schedule was rougher and some of the stars were a mite slow getting into shape.

A column caught Remo's eye. The writer was berating the Eagles' annual open tryout, scheduled for today as a publicity farce.

"The Eagles will have the cameras and the newsmen, the fanfare and the fans, but they won't have any football players. They are preying on the secret fantasy of many American men, who imagine themselves running for a touchdown before thousands of screaming fans, when the hard fact is that professional football players are reared from high school to be professional athletes of abnormal size and speed, and if a search were made across the entire country, probably not one person could be found who could make the Eagles' taxi squad. Today's open tryouts are a cruel farce and this reporter, for one, will not cover them.

"If the television stations and other news media, such as my own newspaper, would do the same, we would see an end to this free agent hoax. The only thing the Eagles are really trying out is our gullibility. So far, they seem to be successful."

Remo looked around the almost empty bus station. It reeked of disinfectant as all bus stations in the wee hours reek of disinfectant. He stuffed the paper into a trash can. It would be foolish for him to go to the Eagles' training camp at Pell College, just outside the city limits. For one thing, he was supposed to go to great lengths to avoid publicity and second, what would he prove? He was in an entirely different business from professional athletes. And for three, Smith would be phoning him that morning for a meeting in Atlanta. That had been the point of the telegram about Aunt Mildred. And for four, Chiun frowned upon unnecessary displays. Those were four excellent reasons not to take a look at the Eagle training camp. Besides, he had gotten rid of his football lusts in high school. Middle guards simply didn't weigh less than two hundred pounds, not even in college. Remo went to the water cooler and filled his mouth again. They were four excellent reasons not to go.

The fare to Pell College was $7.35 and Remo gave the cab driver a ten and told him to keep the change. It was just 6:30 A.M. and already a line had begun to form outside the field house. At just shy of six feet, Remo was one of the shortest men in line. He was also one of the lightest.

Remo stood in line behind a garage mechanic who played semipro and said he knew he didn't have a chance but he just wanted to butt heads once or twice with real pros. He had played against the Eagles' third string linebacker once in high school and had gotten by him once. Of course, he had been hit so hard he had fumbled four other times during the game.

On Remo's other side was a college dropout of six-feet-seven, 280 pounds, who had never played football but thought he might show enough talent, considering his size. The men

28

gathered and the line grew. All of the men but one cherished fantasies most men had surrendered in childhood. That one's mouth tasted of salt and he was experiencing a body and mind change hundreds upon hundreds of years old, a transformation never experienced before by anyone outside the little Korean village of Sinanju.

The assistant coaches avoided the eyes of the free agents as they broke them down into groups. The only thing the coaches seemed concerned with were the release forms. Seven for each man, freeing the Eagles from responsibility for any possible injuries.

The hopefuls were herded to the sidelines of the Pell playing field and told to wait. The Eagles went through their morning workout. They did not exchange any words with the amateurs. When a television crew arrived, five applicants were called from the sidelines. Remo was not one of them. He was too small, according to an assistant coach.

"They're putting them in with the regulars," said a man sitting next to Remo. "I was here last year."

"Why don't they give them a chance and put them in with the rookies," asked Remo.

"Rookies would kill 'em. A rookie will hit anything that moves, just to show they can hit. Rookies are dangerous. The regulars will take it easy on us."

For each television crew and reporter, another group of free agents was trotted out. Remo waited through the morning workout, but was not called. At lunch they all ate with Eagles but at separate tables. Every now and then, one of the applicants was called to sit near an Eagle. One photographer had an Eagle feed an applicant, holding the fork near his mouth and smiling at the camera. When the photographer said, "Got it," the offensive tackle dropped the forkful of coleslaw in the other man's lap. The man tried to laugh it off.

One of the reporters tried to get Lerone Marion Bettee, aka "The Animal," to pose with an applicant's head in his hands. Bettee refused, saying he did not use his hands like that without toilet paper.

Remo made a mental note that a man like Bettee didn't really know what to do with his hands and therefore had no use for them.

The middle linebacker of the Eagles, who was known as one of the toughest in the business and had been quoted as saying "anyone who doesn't like to hit and be hit shouldn't play pro ball," came over to the applicants' table and asked them how they liked their lunch. He volunteered that pro football was really hard work and sometimes he wished he could make his living at something else. This broke the ice and other players came over to chat but the head coach broke it up, saying the players were there for work, not socializing.

Lerone Marion Bettee, six-foot-six, 267 pounds, and built like a clothes hamper, complained loudly that the players should never have spoken to the applicants because the applicants belonged in the stands, not on the playing field or in the players' dining room.

By mid-afternoon when all the newsmen had gone, Remo and another man had still not played. An assistant coach told them to come back next year and that they would now be given an Eagle pennant as a souvenir.

30

"I came to play and I'm going to play," said Remo.

"Tryout day is over."

"Not for me," said Remo. "I'm not going until I get a chance."

"It's over."

"Not for me."

The assistant coach trotted to the head coach, who shrugged, mumbled a few words, and sent the assistant coach back to Remo.

"Okay. Get out there at cornerback. We'll run an off-tackle play and you can stand on the field. Don't get in the way of the runner if he should get by Bettee, because you'll get hurt."

"I play middle guard," said Remo. "I played it in high school."

"You can't go into the pit. You won't get out in one piece."

"I want to play middle guard," said Remo.

"Look. So far, no one has gotten hurt real bad. Don't spoil our record."

"I'm playing middle guard," said Remo and trotted out to the scrimmage line. For the first time in football history a real killer was on a football field. If the coach had known what was really entering the scrimmage, he would have locked his team up in Fort Knox to protect them. But all he saw was a little nuisance, so he waved to his offensive center and right guard to gently box in the intruder on the next play so everyone could get back to work.

Remo got down in the four-point stance he had learned in high school, but it now felt unnatural for his body. It was a bad placement of the centrality of his being, so he stood up. His shoulders barely topped the crouching center and guard, who were just an arm's height from the playing surface.

The cleats felt unnatural on the hard-packed summer grass so Remo kicked them off. He could smell the sharp sweat of bodies before him and even the meat on their breath. The quarterback who looked so small on television was a good four inches taller than Remo. The center snapped the ball, the quarterback rammed it into the stomach of Bobby Joe Hooker, whose bulk churned to right tackle. Center Raymond Wolsczak and guard Herman Doffman rose to gently box in the little man in stocking feet, lest he get between the runner Hooker and the defensive tackle, Bettee, and wind up in the hospital. Or the morgue.

But as they moved, the little man was not there. Doffman felt something brush by him and so did the quarterback. Hooker felt the ball hit his stomach as the quarterback handed off, and then felt what he later described as a sledgehammer in the stomach and somehow the intruder was casually trotting toward the goal line with the football tucked under his arm, straight-arming imaginary opponents. Remo Williams, Weequahic High School middle guard, who had never even made all-Newark.

"He slugged me," gasped Hooker, pointing at the quarterback from his kneeling position. "He slugged me."

"All right. You with the football," yelled the head coach. "Give it back and get your pennant."

"This is a tryout," said Remo, returning for scrimmage. "I'm not going until you prove to me I haven't made the team. Just once, prove it," said the former Weequahic mediocre.

"Okay," said the head coach, a tall man whose

paunch filled out a white sweat shirt at girth. "Wolsczak and Doffman, move the little guy already. Same play. Off tackle. Hooker, get off your damned knees."

"I can't move, coach," said Hooker.

"Well then, run it out, Hooker," yelled the coach and the trainer and water boy helped him from the field. "You there. Bettee. What are you doing lining up behind the middle guard? You're the left tackle, dummy."

With a grunt, and a malicious smile, Lerone Marion Bettee sidestepped to the left but kept his eye on the frail, shoeless middle guard.

"Leave him alone," the all-pro middle linebacker whispered to Bettee and when the ball was snapped, he blocked Bettee, his own defensive teammate, to stop him from pulverising the little guy without shoes.

The caution was not needed.

There was the amateur, wiggling down the field again and second-string fullback Bull Throck was on his face, three yards behind the line of scrimmage. Doffman was holding his shoulder and wincing in pain and the center was still looking for his blocking assignment.

"What is the matter with you?" yelled the head coach. This time he called for a right side sweep and Lerone Marion Bettee couldn't wait for the little man without shoes to get in his way. But all he saw was the flash of white socks and Willie Jeeter scurrying around the right side of the line was dumped precisely two yards behind the line of scrimmage. Jeeter did better than the fullbacks. He held on to the ball.

By the fourth play, five men had been injured and the little fellow in white socks had made four tackles in a row, two of them stealing the ball.

The head coach, known for his shrewdness in judging talent, began to suspect he might have something here. He promptly bawled out an assistant coach for not spotting the guy earlier.

"You," he yelled at Remo. "What's your name?"

"Doesn't matter," said Remo, whose mouth was again deliciously free of salt. "I'll take my pennant now and go."

Remo walked toward the sidelines and the coach yelled out, "Stop that man," which was all Lerone Marion Bettee had to hear. With awesome speed for his overpowering bulk, Bettee was charging across the field to clip the little fellow from behind. But what Bettee did not realize was that every man, and especially someone of his size, creates air pressure when he runs and while most people, especially those with eyesight, are not sensitive to those pressures, the frail little guard was sensitive even unto his muscle fibers. Bettee plowed down into the man and kept on plowing into the ground. The man kept walking away. Bettee's right forearm, which had been a weapon of war in the National Football League, was numb. It would remain that way for eighteen months. Bettee lay on the ground paralyzed. In a week, he would be able to move his head, and in a month, he would begin to walk again.

"You there, Bettee," yelled the coach. "Run it out."

He turned to one of the assistant coaches. "Well, we got that little fellow signed anyhow."

"All we have are liability releases, coach. You said we shouldn't waste the other forms on the tryouts."

"You're fired," said the coach. He scrambled across the field after Remo. He said the young

34

man showed promise and since the coach liked him and he seemed to be a real team player and the team could go all the way this year, he was offering Remo a chance to get in on the ground floor. The minimum contract, which left him all that wonderful room for salary growth.

Remo shook his head. He shook his head as he put on his street clothes, all the way through three final offers, the last two of which the coach assured him priced him out of the National Football League.

"We can always draft you and then you go nowhere."

"Draft away," said Remo. "You don't even know my name."

"Yes, we do," said the coach, looking at a release form. "We have your signature, Abraham, and you're ours. You really are. Now be reasonable, Mr. Lincoln. You've eaten our food, soiled our uniforms, you owe us something."

Back at the hotel, Smith was furious. He sat stone-faced as Remo entered. Chiun was watching his daytime serials. Remo and Smith went into the bedroom, so as not to disturb the Master of Sinanju.

"Chiun seems to think your disappearance when you were supposed to be here is some sort of a progression," said Smith. "I consider it undependable."

"Have an Eagle pennant," Remo said.

"I hope you're happy," Smith said. "Because you are going to bodyguard someone whom we are not even sure is alive, whose whereabouts we do not know, and who has to be guarded against assassins we do not know."

"Your unparalleled intelligence service is up to par, Smitty," said Remo.

"We have one lead," Smith said. "One possibility. What do you know about acid rock?"

"It's loud," Remo said.

CHAPTER THREE

"I don't like that kind of music," said Willie "The Bomb" Bombella.

Morris Edelstein made sure the intercom that connected him to his secretary was off. For a little final security he ran a small metal detector around his office walls again. He locked his telephone in his top desk drawer which was lined with lead, because, as anyone knew, even a dead telephone receiver could be a line for a bug.

"What're you doing?" asked Willie the Bomb.

"Shut up," said Morris Edelstein.

"You think everyplace is bugged. You'd think your own bathroom was bugged to catch your farts, Mo," said Willie the Bomb.

"It so happens I found a bug in the hamper last year," Edelstein replied.

"The feds?"

"No. My ex-wife. But it could have been anything, anyone."

"You worry a lot, Mo," said Willie the Bomb, and he placed his two giant hands on his massive belly that stretched the middle of his size eighteen extra-large silk shirt. A small gray fedora topped a craggy face made craggier by a scar across his nose, suffered when an union dispute was settled with baseball bats. Against Willie the Bomb's face, the bat finished second. It broke.

Along with its wielder's left arm and back. When the bat-wielder was released from the hospital, he found out something very strange about his front door lock. It did a funny thing when you turned the key. It took off the front of the house.

Police in St. Louis attributed this to a bomb and questioned Willie the Bomb Bombella at length. But Willie said nothing, on advice of his attorney, Mo Edelstein, who triumphed once again over the unfair police harrassment of his client, reinforcing the constitutional concepts of men like Jefferson, Franklin, and Hamilton, and making it possible for at least three St. Louis citizens a year to get surprises when they started their cars, opened their front doors, or peeked into unexpected packages.

"I wanna see my lawyer, Mo Edelstein," were the words used over and over again by Willie the Bomb, who had a good thing going, except for one little flaw. Which was what Edelstein had called him into the office about that morning.

Edelstein locked the metal detector in another drawer and lowered the shades, shutting out what might charitably be called the St. Louis skyline, but more accurately the surviving remnants of a city that went from frontier outpost to slum with barely a pause at civilization.

"First of all, Willie, I am not broaching this subject because I think you like acid rock."

"I don't like it at all," said Willie, "but I own a piece of Vampire Records."

"Which doesn't make you much money, right?"

"It's only a little piece," said Willie.

"I understand," said Mo Edelstein. "You're a good client, Willie."

"Thank you, Mo."

37

"And only one thing would make you a perfect client. One small little thing, Willie."

"What is it, Mo?"

"Do not take offense at this, Willie. Please. But sometimes, Willie, you don't exactly come up with the full bill."

"I pay often," said Willie, leaning forward in his seat.

"You do. You do, Willie, you pay very often. You're one of my most-often paying clients, except for those who pay all the time."

"Nobody's perfect," said Willie.

"Right," said Edelstein. "Not even the people who pay you. I do not mean to cast aspersions on your employers or anything."

"What's an aspersion?"

"A not nice thing, Willie. But you should be a rich man."

"I'm loyal to the people I work for," said Willie and his dark brown eyes narrowed.

"I am not suggesting you betray any of your employers, Willie," said Edelstein, smiling as wide as he could. He wiped the perspiration from his forehead. "I am suggesting a way to make a lot of money. Lots and lots of money. More money, Willie, than you ever made in your whole life."

" 'Cause I wouldn't never betray the people I work for."

"I know you wouldn't, Willie. That's why I'm giving you this great opportunity. How would you like to make almost a million dollars? Do you know how much that is, Willie?"

Willie the Bomb Bombella's eyes rose. He thought very hard. And what he thought was *This man is lying to me.*

"It's a lot," said Willie.

"I'm telling you the truth, Willie. Almost a

38

million dollars. It's waiting out there for you and just a little bit for me. Just what you owe me, Willie. A hundred and twelve thousand dollars."

Willie's eyes opened wider. He nodded. If there was $112,000 in it for Edelstein, maybe this man was not lying to him. When there was so much money for Edelstein in anything, everything seemed to happen.

"My employers have done me some injustices I can think of," said Willie.

"No, no. It has nothing to do with them. I have a second cousin who lives on the West Coast . . ."

"There is nothing worse than blood betraying blood," Willie interrupted.

"No, no, Willie. Listen to me. He is a funeral director. He buried someone recently and a strange thing happened. There was money in a funeral wreath. It was not his money so he did not keep it."

Willie's eyes narrowed. *This man is lying to me,* he thought again.

"He didn't keep it because he was afraid."

Willie nodded. Edelstein might be telling the truth, he thought.

"But a strange thing happened. A voice on the telephone asked him one night if the money had reached the family of the dead man."

Willie nodded and Edelstein continued.

"My cousin is smart. He found out what the money was for. The word is open contract."

Willie's eyes narrowed.

"An open contract. You've heard of a contract on someone's life?" Edelstein paused and laughed nervously. "Of course you have. Well, this is the sort of contract where anyone can fill it and collect the money. See?"

This man is lying to me or setting me up or is a fool. No, thought Willie, Edelstein is no fool.

"You mean you get paid after the job?"

"Right."

"What if no one wants to pay you?"

"I don't think that would happen. Already more than $100,000 has been thrown around for failures. Real money. My second cousin wasn't the only person this happened to. Other funeral directors had the same thing happen. Most of them aren't as smart as my cousin. He got a phone number."

Willie watched Edelstein take a piece of paper from the center desk drawer.

"You get financial details from that number," Edelstein said.

"Did you call this number, Mo?"

"That is not my sort of thing, Willie. I've got to stay here to protect you in case there is any trouble. I should not even tell you that the girl's name is Vickie Stoner, she is nineteen, and she will be at an acid rock concert in Massachusetts in two days, if she is still alive."

Willie blinked. "Let me get this straight. I am supposed to try to do a job on somebody who might not be alive for someone I never saw for money I do not get until the hit is good. Is that what you are telling me, Mo?"

"A million dollars, Willie. A million dollars. Can you think of a million dollars?"

Willie tried to think of a million dollars. He thought of it in cars, in ready cash, in owning pieces of companies, but he could not imagine it. Another thought was crowding it out. *This man may be crazy*.

"I'm not crazy, Willie," said Edelstein. "If it

weren't so strange, why would so much be offered? A million dollars, Willie."

Willie looked at the piece of paper in Edelstein's hand. "How come there's ten numbers?"

"Area code."

"I do not know this area code."

"Chicago."

"Why is it you know the girl's name?"

"My cousin."

"Give me your phone," said Willie, taking the piece of paper from Edelstein's hand.

"No, Willie. Not from here. We don't want that. We don't want our defense lawyer to be connected, because he has to stay free in case something goes wrong. We want to be able to say, 'I want my attorney, Mo Edelstein,' not, 'Guard, I have a message for Inmate 79312.' That's what we want, Willie."

"We want you to come with us," said Willie.

"No, no. That's what we don't want," yelled Edelstein.

"That is what we want," said Willie. As they left the office for a street phone, Mo Edelstein took two Maalox and a Seconal. After the phone conversation, he popped a Nembutal. He was still nervous, so he took a Librium.

"You know, if they put booze in a pill, Mo, you'd be an alcoholic," said Willie the Bomb.

Edelstein's face eased somewhat as he watched Willie the Bomb load his Lincoln Continental. Edelstein's curiosity was aroused. Here was a man with an IQ that probably never saw the high side of retarded, but when it came to making and setting bombs, knowing what they would do and how they would do it, Bombella was the Michelangelo of the blast.

Bombella sensed this newfound respect and

41

although he had never before explained how he did things, he did so for Edelstein. He knew Edelstein would never use his trade secrets. Edelstein could do more, Willie knew, with a briefcase than Al Capone with a thermonuclear warhead.

Going east and north from St. Louis, Willie explained that nothing he had in the car was illegal until he put it together.

"Almost anything that'll burn can be made into a bomb," Willie explained. "What a bomb is, is really a very fast fire with not enough place to go fast enough."

"That is the most brilliant explanation I have ever heard of a bomb," said Edelstein. "Brilliant in its simplicity."

"Now there are two basic ways to use one. One is to use it to send something else into the hit or another is to make the hit part of this very fast burning fire. Now, take a car for instance. Most of these guys go putting it in the engine. Do you know why?"

"No," said Edelstein.

"Cause they only know how to hook up to the ignition and they don't want no one to see the wires. Right in the engine they put it and sometimes it works and sometimes it doesn't. You know why it doesn't. It doesn't cause there's a frigging fire wall between the driver and the engine and all you get sometimes is blowing off some poor guy's legs."

"Incompetent," said Edelstein, who secretly despised prosecutors who did not give him a good professional battle.

"Yeah, that," said Bombella, knowing from the tone of the voice that incompetence was something not nice. "Now the place to put a bomb is under the seat. You use a mechanical

42

device that works on pressure, maybe eighty pounds pressure tops, no more."

"But who weighs that little?"

"Some guys slide in and you get the torso."

"But some torsos must weigh less, especially women's," Edelstein said.

"The brake does it. The brake drives the body into the seat, so you're guaranteed your blast at the first stop."

"Brilliant," said Edelstein. "But then why did you use the ignition last May."

"I didn't do the job last May," said Bombella.

"Funny," said Edelstein. "That's what you told me then too."

"Now for a car I don't like to use no material like metal shards, nails, or a hand grenade kind of thing. I like a clean explosion. Especially in the summer, when the windows are up for air conditioning. The whole car acts like a casing."

"Brilliant," said Edelstein.

"The air pressure created is amazing. It'd take off someone even without breaking 'em up. Just by the concussion."

"Brilliant," said Edelstein.

"I could make a bomb out of a pack of cards," said Bombella. "You see that tree there? I could take it off exactly where you want it and land it where you want it. You could put a home plate anywheres near that tree and I'd get you a strike."

"Can you throw a curve?" asked Edelstein, jesting.

"Nah. I can't do that yet," said Willie, after thinking a moment. "But if it was a wet day with some heavy air and if we had a good wind, maybe eighteen to twenty-three miles an hour, and it was kind of a good-shaped tree like a young

43

maple, and you let me put the plate where I wanted, I might be able to get a strike on a curve."

"You're beautiful, Willie."

They drove leisurely, and a day and a half later neared Pittsfield, Mass., the general area of the rock festival where Vickie Stoner was to show up.

"Is this the right way?" Edelstein said.

"A little detour I was told about when I made that phone call," Bombella said. Outside Pittsfield, Willie stopped the Continental near a large sign that read Whitewood Cottages. He went to a mailbox and took out a package that looked like a rolled magazine. The computer printed name on it said "Edelstein."

"I'm not supposed to be involved like this," said Edelstein when Willie returned to the car. "What's in the package."

"It's supposed to be money and a note."

"I'll read the note to you," said Edelstein.

"I can read," said Willie. And he could. Edelstein watched the lips move as Willie the Bomb formed words. Edelstein tried to get a peek at the letters pasted on the paper, but Willie defensively shielded the note.

"Count the money," said Willie, tossing the package to Edelstein and slipping the note into his pocket.

"Fifty thousand," said Edelstein.

"A lot of money," said Willie. "Give it to me."

"It's half of what you owe me," said Edelstein.

"I'll give you everything at the music show. There'll be some money there for us."

"And then perhaps I might sort of leave cause you don't really need me, right, Willie. I'd only get in the way."

44

"Right," said Willie glumly. "You want to see something really great in the way of bombs?"

"What is it?" asked Edelstein suspiciously.

As they passed a country store, Willie suggested Edelstein get a jar of Prosco homemade pickles and, as he suspected, Edelstein couldn't open the bottle. They drove on through Pittsfield with Willie refusing to stop for lunch and Edelstein eyeing the pickles sitting there unopened between them.

"I could blow the top off that jar," boasted Willie, as they sped down Route 8 to North Adams.

"Really?"

"Bet your ass I could. I could blow it clean off without even a crack in the glass."

"Do it now, Willie. I'm starved."

Willie pulled over to the gravel shoulder of the road, reached into the back seat of the car and from under a magazine removed the bomb made of playing cards. Into its side he pressed a penlike device and where it protruded he very carefully wrapped a straightened paper clip into a coil.

"Get out of the car," said Willie and when Edelstein had stretched himself outside the car, Willie handed him the jar of pickles. "Hold this in your left hand."

Edelstein took it in both hands.

"Left hand," said Willie, and Edelstein took the jar in his left hand.

Willie thought a moment, then said, "Put the pickles on the rock over there."

When Edelstein had and returned to the car, Willie gave him the bomb.

"Now do this just right," he said. "Put the part with the paperclip on top of the jar, then

45

walk back. Don't wait. It will start when I start the car."

"Brilliant. How does that work?"

"Just do it," said Willie, and Edelstein scampered back to the rock, his shoes spitting gravel behind him.

He gingerly dropped the bomb on the jar and ran back to the car.

"Okay. Start it, genius. I'm hungry."

"You didn't put the clip against the top of the jar."

"How could you see?"

"I know. Watch. I'll start the car and nothing will happen," and Willie turned the ignition and sure enough the jar of pickles and the bomb were there.

"Well, I'll be. You're a genius."

Edelstein went back to the jar of pickles, picked up the bomb, and even though it wouldn't balance that way, pressed the paperclip against the metal top of the jar.

And within an instant his stomach was filled with pieces of pickles and glass shards and the metal jar cap. So was what was left of his face.

The glass shards spit, cracking into the side of the car and even making a nick in the windows. They shouldn't have.

"Frigging Prosco pickles," said Willie the Bomb Bombella. "They're subcontracting out their jars again to those cheapie manufacturers."

And he drove off along the road toward the rock concert, where he hoped to be able to cash in on the million dollar open contract himself. The $50,000 in his pocket had been for a side job. As the note had said: "Kill Edelstein. He talks too much."

46

CHAPTER FOUR

Vickie Stoner was alive and rapping on the side of Route 8 just outside Pittsfield when she could have sworn she heard an explosion down the road.

"It's the revolution," wheezed one of the boys, a lanky blond with shoulder-length hair wrapped tight around his forehead with an Indian band that somehow combined the signs of the Mohawk and Arapaho, an accomplishment that eluded history but not Dibble manufacturing of Boise, Idaho.

"Not now. Maggot's at North Adams," said Vickie. "I'm going to ball Maggot."

"Maggot's bitchen," said another young girl, her legs straddling a knapsack. They had been waiting in the Berkshires' morning sun for hours, as processions of bicycles, painted Volkswagen buses, and straight cars passed them by. Some of the girls suggested they were passed up because the boys didn't paint the signs with the right karma. The boys said it was because the girls didn't get up on the side of the road and do some work.

"Like what?" asked Vickie.

"Show a boob or something," said one of the boys.

"You show a boob," one of the girls said defensively.

"I don't have one."

"Then show what you've got."

"I'd get busted, man."

"Well, I'm not getting up there like some piece of meat."

So in the early afternoon, they waited for transportation just twelve miles short of the end of their journey—the rock festival known as the North Adams Experience. The town may have claimed it as its own. The promoters may have claimed the profits. But the experience belonged to those who would be part of it. You didn't attend it like some movie, sitting in a seat and letting the screen lay all sorts of stuff on you. You were part of it and it was part of you and you made it what it was with the Dead Meat Lice and the Hamilton Locomotives and the Purloined Letters.

It wouldn't begin at eight o'clock that night like the ads said. It had already begun. Coming to it was part of it. The wheels were part of it. Sitting on the side of the road waiting for a ride was part of it. The pills and pouches and the little envelopes were part of it. You were part of it. It was your thing and no one else could tell you what it was, man, especially if they tried.

Vickie Stoner refused to discuss whether the loud noise was the beginning of the revolution, a world war or a car backfiring. She had had enough of that crap, man. Up to here and beyond.

The whole thing was a bummer, all the problems with her father and now all the mess of the past few days.

It had started simply too. A simple, reasonable, nonnegotiable demand. All she had wanted was Maggot. She had had Nells Borson of the Cockamamies, all of the Hindenburgh Seven and what she needed, really needed, all she needed, was Maggot.

But when she told her father, he had locked her

in their Palm Beach home. That coffin with lawns. That slammer with butlers. So she split and was brought back. She split again and was brought back again.

All right, daddy wanted to negotiate. She'd negotiate. She got these papers and ripped off some of the tapes her daddy made of all his telephone conversations and she had said:

"You wanna deal? Let's deal. What will you give me for the papers and tapes on the grain deal? What am I bid? I'm bid. I'm bid. I'm bid. Do I hear laying off me? Do I hear laying off me? What do I hear? I'm bid. I'm bid."

"Go to your room, Victoria," was the bid, so Vickie Stoner pretended to go upstairs and then she split. With the tapes and papers, which she took to the U.S. Attorney's office in Miami. And what a trip it was. All of Daddy's friends, all of them, with lawyers, nervous breakdowns and sudden excursions around the world, saying how could anyone do anything like that. That was a high all right, but then the straights started laying it on her and this guy Blake was all right, but he was a downer.

And then Denver and that crap on the balcony and in the room and the bad vibes, man. So she just split again and here she was on the side of Route 8, waiting for the last few miles of the North Adams Experience. And down the road, maybe that crap was starting again.

"It's the revolution," said the boy with the Indian head band.

But he had said that the night before when the pop bottle fell and cracked open, and when they saw a squadron of jets overhead, he said it was the fascist pigs going to bomb Free Bedford Stuyvesant.

49

"Just keep the sign moving," said Vickie, and she rested her head on her knapsack, and hoped her father did not worry too much about her. At least, though, when she talked to him now, he was becoming reasonable.

A gray Lincoln Continental with a real straight at the wheel breezed by them and Vickie closed her eyes. Suddenly, there was a screeching of tires. A brief silence. The car backed up.

Vickie opened her eyes. He was an ugly straight, all right, with a big scar across his nose and he was looking down at something, then back at Vickie, and down at that thing which he then put into his pocket.

"Youse want a lift?" he yelled through a lowered car window. Funny-looking car, all marks on the right side of it, like someone had gone at it with fifty nails or something.

"Right on," said the boy with the Indian headband and they all piled into the luxurious car with Vickie last.

"You're Mafia, aren't you?" said the boy with the headband.

"Why you wanna say something like that?" said the driver, his eyes on Vickie in the rearview mirror. "That's not nice."

"I'm all for the Mafia. The Mafia represents the struggle against the establishment. It is the culmination of hundreds of years of struggle against oppressive government."

"I ain't Mafia. There's no such thing," said Willie the Bomb, his eyes still on Vickie, his brain now convinced he had found the right girl. "Where you kids gonna sleep?"

"We're not going to sleep. We're going to be. At the North Adams Experience."

"Out in the air you're gonna sleep?"

"Under the stars, if the government hasn't fucked that up too."

"Youse kids, I like. You know the best place to sleep?"

"In a hayloft?"

"No," said Willie the Bomb Bombella. "Under a maple tree. A nice, straight maple tree. It absorbs the bad things from the air. It really does. You sleep under a maple tree and you're never gonna forget it. Really. I swear to God."

CHAPTER FIVE

"Is he somebody?" shrieked a blotch-faced girl whose bouncing boobs were causing a great commotion underneath her tie-dyed tee shirt.

"He's nobody," said Remo, fishing for his motel room key. Chiun sat on the other side of his fourteen large, lacquered trunks. His golden morning kimono wafted gently westward with a breeze that blew across the North Adams Experience, or what had been Farmer Tyrus's north forty until he had suddenly discovered it could be used for something even more valuable than not growing corn.

"He looks like somebody."

"He's a nobody."

"Can I have a piece of that way-out shirt he's wearing?"

"I wouldn't touch it if I were you," said Remo.

"He wouldn't mind if I took just a little piece of his dashiki. Oh, he's somebody. He's somebody.

51

I know it. Hey, everybody. Somebody. Somebody's here."

From cars they came and from the backs of trucks they came. From behind rocks they came and around trees they came. First a few and then, when the mass movement from Tyrus's field was noticed, more followed. Someone was here. Someone was here. The high point of every rock event. Somebody to see.

Remo went into the motel room. There were several possible outcomes to this sudden rush, one of them involved the probable need to dispose of bodies.

But why not? Why should anything go right, starting now? It had begun badly at the briefing session with Smith, which had bordered on the absurd. First, there had been the girl, Vickie Stoner. Her photograph taken at her debut, her baby pictures, a picture of her in a crowd, a picture of her with her eyes glazed.

It was Remo's job to protect her from unknown killers. That is, if she was still alive. She might be at the bottom of some lake now, or buried in a cave, or beneath a house, or decomposed in acid—the decomposing kind or the other kind.

But if she was alive, where would she be? Well, no one knew, least of all her father, but there was a pretty good theory that she would be at a rock festival somewhere, because she was a groupie type.

Which rock festival? Chances were she would not miss the North Adams Experience if she were alive. After all, Maggot and the Dead Meat Lice were playing there. How many people would be there? From four hundred to one hundred thousand.

Thanks a lot.

Remo had then posed this question to Smith: Since the open contract had obviously come from one of the people involved in the Russian grain deal, possibly even Vickie's father, why not let Remo do what he did best? Go down the list of suspects, find the one putting up the money, and reason with him.

No good, Smith explained. It would take too much time and it had too many flaws in it. Suppose Remo went after the wrong man. The right man could get Vickie Stoner. No. Protecting her was the answer.

So that was that and here he was.

There was a commotion outside the motel room and then the door opened and Chiun's trunks started coming in with acid freaks yanking at their handles, moaning and straining as if they were in chains. Remo heard yelling. He went to the window. A very fat young man whose belly was exploding over blue jeans and whose shirt had a peace symbol on it was swinging at a girl whose shirt said *Love, not War*. She was clawing at his testicles.

"I'm gonna carry his trunk. He said I could," yelled the girl.

"He said *I* could."

"He said *I* could."

"No, me. You fat pig shit."

And so it went in many couples until Remo observed that Chiun might become worried about the safety of his trunks. Chiun rose and stood above one trunk, his hands extended, the long nails reaching to the heavens. And he spoke to them, these children, as Remo saw them. And what he said was that their hearts should be in concurrence with the forces of the universe and

53

they should be one with that which was one. They should be all with that which is all.

They should be as one hand and one back and one body. The trunks should rise like swans on gilded lakes. The green one first.

And thus it came to pass that morning that the trunks, one by one, went into the room of the Master of Sinanju. The green one first.

And when all the trunks were in the room, piled one on another, the green one separate by the window, the Master of Sinanju bade them all farewell. And when they did not wish to leave such an illustrious one, insisting he tell them the somebody he was, he no longer spoke. But a strange thing began to happen. The golden swirls of the kimono rustled, and one and another and another of these followers found themselves hurled out, until the last one, he too, was outside the door. With an ugly welt on his cheek.

"He is somebody," shrieked a girl. "Only somebody would act that way. I've got to have him. I've got to have him. I want him."

Chiun opened the green trunk. In it, Remo knew, was the special television set that not only showed one channel, but taped two other networks simultaneously, because as Chiun had often said, all the good shows were on at once, the good shows being the soap operas.

Another special feature of the set was that all the Sony marks had been ground, pried, or painted off, and replaced with *Made in Korea*. Chiun refused to use Japanese because of what he described as a recent treacherous incident committed by the Japanese against the House of Sinanju. By going through a chart of Japanese emperors Remo had deduced that the recent incident had occurred in 1282 A.D.

According to Chiun, the Japanese emperor, hearing of the wisdom and wonder of Sinanju, had sent an emissary to the then Master of Sinanju, requesting guidance in a difficult matter. Little did the Master realize what treachery, what perfidy he was dealing with, for after giving his assistance, he realized something had been stolen. Agents of the emperor had been watching him in his tasks and they had copied his methods, thus stealing the art of Ninji, or silent night attack, from Sinanju.

"So they paid for a hit and copied some techniques," Remo had said.

"They stole that which lasts longer than rubies," said Chiun. "They stole wisdom, which I attempt to give to you and which you treat as nothing."

"How do you figure that, Little Father?"

"You do not appreciate the perfidy of the Japanese. It is good that they do not get their hands on this television set, lest they would copy that too. You cannot trust the Japanese."

"Yeah, they could rip off the whole great Korean electronics industry if the Koreans aren't careful."

When *As the Planet Revolves* came on, Remo went outside to see if he could find a red-headed girl of nineteen who might or might not be alive.

As Remo moved through the crowd outside the door, he heard comments of "That's nobody, he works for somebody . . . hey, stop pushing . . . hey, watch your hands . . . that's nobody . . . he's nobody . . . somebody's still inside."

He roamed the field of Farmer Tyrus amid the wafting odor of marijuana and hashish. He stepped over couples and knapsacks. At the edge of the field he avoided the tangle of cables

55

pushing toward a raised stage where summer squash once grew. Two tall metal towers flanked the stage. An army of electricians moved with disciplined energy, checking and installing equipment. Only their beards and clothes seemed casual.

Near the stage, Remo spotted violently-red hair flowing over a knapsack. A brown-haired head was pressed to it. Both bodies were under a blanket and moving.

He bypassed two girls, helping a third who was coming out of a bad LSD trip. He went to the moving blanket and waited. And waited. He could not see the face under the red hair, so he waited some more. When he was tired of waiting, he bent down quickly and sent his two forefingers vibrating down the base of the spine of the uppermost body. He did it so quickly it looked as if he were picking a leaf off the blanket.

"Oooooh," groaned the top body in ecstasy, as Remo had expected, but the movement under the blanket did not cease.

Enough was enough. He pushed aside the short brown hair to see the face that belonged to the long red hair. It was not Vickie Stoner. It was not Vickie anyone. The her was a him and the real her was on top with the short brown hair.

"Do it again like you did before," she said. Remo went off to look for Vickie Stoner, if she were still alive. He checked the field and he checked the painted buses along the road. Every so often, he asked the question:

"I'm looking for my woman. Nineteen. Red hair. Freckles. Name's Vickie."

But there was no response. Then a gray Lincoln Continental passed him. A scarfaced man was at the wheel. Sleeping in the back was a red-haired

56

girl with a glory of freckles. It could be. Remo saw the Continental find a parking spot a half mile down the road. Four young people and the man with the scar emerged and walked the rest of the way to the North Adams Experience. The heavyset man with the scar seemed very friendly, gesturing to the tower on the left of the bandstand. He even cleared a place for the group, roughly pushing other young people out of the way. Remo followed.

"I heard somebody is in the motel," said the redhead excitedly. It *was* Vickie Stoner.

Now, how could word reach so quickly, Remo wondered. He had heard that in the acid culture rumors traveled faster than light, and with surprising accuracy.

"He's somebody but we don't know who," said a young blond man with an Indian headband. Remo noticed by the way he stood what no one else had noticed, because they could only recognize a weapon from its outlines, not from the way a body reacted to carrying it. Remo knew the young blond man with the headband was armed and he was watching Vickie Stoner.

The heavyset man with the gray fedora was eyeing the left tower. He did not stand armed. But Remo could feel something strange about the way the man looked at that tower, as if he were examining it for some destructive use.

Remo sat down by Vickie Stoner, not even speaking to her. He just waited. Tyrus's field filled. There were echoes to greetings and calls, the twang of an occasional guitar.

One loud amateur voice wafted over the field, and as Remo watched Vickie Stoner fall asleep, he tried to discern the lyrics the voice was singing.

"Pie wide, sucking on a cloudstick,

Whirl the long road,
Happy tears and good-bye beers,
Drop tomorrow like yesterday's trip tick,
Pie wide, sucking on a cloudstick.
Rip your belly with chemical love.
They're driving you downward,
With Christ's rummage sale.
Pie wide. She does it like she loves it.
Pie wide, sucking on a cloudstick."

Remo asked the blond boy with the headband the meaning of the lyrics.

"It is, man. What it is, it is. You don't define it, dig?"

"Certainly," Remo said.

"It's protest."

"Against what?"

"Everything, man, dig? This fucked-up environment. The hypocrisy. The oppression."

"You like electric guitars?" Remo asked.

"The baddest."

"Do you know where electricity comes from?"

"Good karma, man."

"Generators," Remo said. "Generators. Air polluting, high faluting, generators."

"I never heard that one, man."

"Which one?"

"The lyric. That's a freak, man. Bitchen. Generators, air polluting, high faluting, generators. Baddest."

So Remo, unable to discourse in this language, shut up. He watched the man with the scar fiddle around one tower support and then another, but in such a casual way it looked as if he were just lounging around.

The Dead Meat Lice were to start at seven P.M. At six-thirty, it was announced over the loudspeakers, which could have cut through a swamp, that there would be a forty-five minute delay. At seven P.M., there was an announcement of an hour's delay. At eight-thirty, it was announced any minute now. At nine P.M., as a few harsh floodlights lit the periphery of the area, separating it from the darkness beyond, it was announced: "Here they come."

There was screaming and groaning but they didn't come until ten P.M. When, under a large spotlight, a gallows was raised on the stage. Out of the blackness behind the spot swung a body on a rope. It twitched as though it were being hanged, if hanging required pelvic action similar to coitus. Then the rope seemed to break, and the body landed on its feet, alive in a skin-tight white jumpsuit cut in a wide V to the pubic hairs. Pieces of meat hung from the white satin suit, and already blood was seeping into the shiny material.

A microphone rose from the stage to man height, and Maggot spoke.

"Hello animals. You're dirt. Dirt waits in the field," he yelled. This was greeted by cheers. In the cheering, Remo noticed the blond man with the Indian headband make his move. The weapon he had been carrying was a small-handled ice pick. Only Remo saw it move toward Vickie Stoner, who was slowly awakening next to Remo. Remo moved on the pick. He shattered the driving wrist with his left hand and spun the boy around. The youngster's eyes widened with surprise, first at the numbness in his attacking hand, and then at what was happening at his heart. Nothing was happening. It wasn't beating. It was jelly. He collapsed, spitting internal blood, as the crowd obliviously cheered on.

The Dead Meat Lice crawled and tumbled onto

59

the stage. There was a drummer who doubled as the beater of the gong. In a round enclosure from the right stage rose a piano, organ, and clavichord, with another Dead Meat Louse seated in the middle. A frowzy-headed man with two wind instruments pulled himself up onstage. The crowd cheered the arrival of all three Lice.

Maggot waved his arm and they sang. They sang what Remo made out to be:

"Bedred, mother-racking, tortoise, humpanny, rah, rah, humpanny, mother-racking, bedstead, rackluck."

"Bitchen," screamed Vickie Stoner in Remo's ear, and then the tower to their left gave a wiggle with an explosive pop, then another pop, and people were falling from it and it was coming down like a sledgehammer right where Vickie Stoner was jumping up and down, screaming along with everyone else.

The crowd would hamper free movement, so Remo grabbed Vickie like a loaf of bread and drove his way through bodies to what he felt would be the safest place. The tower came *whoomphing* down, eight tons of it, crushing a ten-yard-wide stretch of people with a heavy, dull splat.

Remo and Vickie were safe. They were at the base of the tower, where it had blown off its foundations head high, just where the big man with the scarred face had been casually moving his hands around.

"Bedred, mother-racking, tortoise humpanny, rah, rah, rah, humpanny, bedstead rackluck."

"They're going on," someone shrieked. "They're going on."

"Dead Meat Lice go on and on. Rule forever, Dead Meat Lice," yelled Maggot, and this was

60

met by cheers blanketing the moans of the victims of the tower.

"Rule forever, Dead Meat Lice," yelled Vickie Stoner. Remo grabbed her by the neck and trundled her off the periphery of the field and out through the gate, where people were not taking money anymore.

"Getcha paws off me, pig," yelled Vickie Stoner, but Remo kept her moving.

"Get offa me," yelled Vickie. She stopped yelling when she saw where she was being taken. She was going to the motel door where "somebody" was.

"He wants me, right?" she gasped. "He sent for me, right? Somebody sent for me. Who is he? You can't say, right? Oh, you have a key. A key to his room. You have a key to *His* room."

Remo no longer had to hold her by the neck. Vickie Stoner jumped up and down excitedly.

"I thought you were going to do a job on me," she said. "I didn't know. I've had Nels Borson. You know Nels Borson? I had him. I had him good. And I had the Hindenburghs. Right at the airport. They were waiting to leave. I had them all."

Remo opened the door, and when Vickie Stoner saw the wisp of an imperial-looking Oriental in midnight-blue kimono sitting on a mat, meditating, she emitted a little excited groan.

Remo shut the door.

"Oh, heavy, heavy, heavy. Rule over all. Rule forever," she said, and knelt before Chiun. Chiun allowed imperious recognition that something was in his presence. Overwhelmed by the slow, arrogant movement, Vickie Stoner pressed her forehead into the mat.

"From the youth of your country, you should learn," said Chiun to Remo.

"Wait'll you find out what she wants."

"You're the baddest," sighed Vickie.

"This little girl already knows more than you, Remo."

"Rule over all," said Vickie.

"And she perceives my proper place."

"Who are you?"

"The Master of Sinanju."

"Fuh-reak out. Sinanju. Bitchen Sinanju, man."

"See, Remo?"

"She doesn't know what you're talking about, Little Father. She hasn't heard of Sinanju. Maybe a half-dozen people alive know Sinanju, and they don't talk about it."

"Diamonds are not more valuable because everyone has them," said Chiun.

"Good night," said Remo, and went to the bathroom to see if he could find some cotton for his ears, knowing that would not help because the vibrations of Maggot and the Dead Meat Lice carried through the walls and the floor of the motel.

Outside, Willie the Bomb Bombella sat in his Continental, an artist frustrated, a craftsman who sees pernicious fate destroy his work. The tower went right. It went fine. It went beautifully. But then along the edge of the crowd was the little red-headed broad with the big mouth and the faggy looking guy with the thick wrists. She was alive. A million dollars from Willie. Right out of the mouths of Willie's children, he had stolen it. Right out of Willie's mattress at home, he had stolen it. Like he had broken into Willie's house or rifled his pockets, he had stolen it.

62

Willie had to get even, despite the fact that they were in a motel with such shoddy structure that the retaining walls hardly retained, and what held it together was sometimes the plaster. There was nothing really good to work against, like brick, or even wood. Wood was good. It gave you splinters like a hand grenade if you did it right. But what was this motel? It was nothing. Might as well blow up an empty field. It gave the creative genius of Willie the Bomb Bombella all the inspiration it needed.

Suppose he handled the motel like an empty field and considered each room a giant gopher hole with gophers as his goal? Perhaps a combination of concussive effect and propelled missiles. He could probably get the girl too. Still make the million.

Willie went to the trunk of his car and started stringing wires, mixing chemicals, and adjusting templates in the small motor device he began to construct. He whistled a tune he had heard in a Walt Disney movie. The tune was "Whistle While you Work."

From the corner of his eye, he saw the door of the thief's room open. It cast a whitish light into the motel parking area. He saw the thief, the guy with the thick wrists who had saved the redhead, walk out. The guy had the nerve to even walk right up to him.

Willie straightened up. He stood almost six inches taller than the little guy and topped him by almost a hundred pounds.

"Whaddaya want?" asked Willie in a tone that in others usually triggered unplanned release of bowels or bladder.

"To break you," Remo said gently.

"What are you talking about?"

"I'm going to break you into little pieces until you beg me to kill you. What are you doing?"

Since Willie had no intention of letting this square squirt walk away, he decided to tell him.

"I'm going to blow you, that little broad, and that gook into next week's garbage."

"Really?" said Remo, honestly interested. "How are you going to do that?"

And Willie explained about his problems with motel construction, his idea about an open field, and how he intended to create a concussive effect to loosen everything, followed by a trio of consecutive explosions that would use the motel debris in a sort of breaking up and burying process.

"That's very tricky," Remo said. "I hope you have the timing devices worked to a very small tolerance."

"That's just it. They ain't. No timing device could be sure to hold. These explosions are set off by the concussion from other explosions, kind of like a chain."

"Nice," Remo said.

"Too bad you ain't gonna feel anything, thief," Willie said, and he clubbed, or thought he clubbed, the side of Remo's head with a swat of his right hand, but his right hand felt funny. It felt as if it were in molten lead, and he found himself lying on the asphalt of the parking lot with the tailpipe of the Continental over his head.

He could feel the vibrations of the Dead Meat Lice against his chest and the oil of the lot was in his nostrils. What seemed like burning lead crawled up his right arm. The pain made him scream and he heard the thief tell him he could stop the burning if he talked, so Willie said he would talk.

"Who were you working with?"

"No one." Something seemed to split the elbow tip into little pieces and Willie screamed again, although nothing had really happened to his elbow. His nerve endings were causing him the awesome pain. Properly manipulated, nerve endings cannot tell the difference between masterful fingers, broken bones, or molten lead.

"I swear, no one."

"What about the blond kid?"

"I was only told to do the job on the redhead."

"Then he wasn't working with you?"

"No. He musta been a free-lance."

"Who gave you the job?"

"Just a voice on the phone. A Chicago number. Oww, stop that. Stop that on my elbow. I'm talking. Jeez, what are you, a pain freak or something? I'm talking. This voice said go to a mailbox."

"Is that all?"

"No, he said that Vickie Stoner was gonna be here and the million dollars was for real."

"What about the mailbox?" Remo asked.

"Well, that was to show good faith," Willie said. "There was fifty thousand there and another assignment for me. The guy I was with. They paid me to do him. Cash. Fifty thousand. Hey, stop it with the elbow."

Willie the Bomb Bombella felt the pain sear his shoulder, then his chest. He tried to answer how the bomb thing really worked but no one understood, really understood. To make the pain stop, he told this bastard how to set off a simple explosion from the materials in his car, and he told him honestly because he would do anything to stop the pain, even die. That would be better. He felt himself trundled into the trunk and then

65

there was darkness as the car bounced along with the bombs banging around his ears and temples. There was one at his right foot and just a tap would set it off and take care of that thief-bastard pain freak.

So Willie tapped his foot.

CHAPTER SIX

Pie wide. She does it like she loves it. Pie wide, sucking on a cloudstick.

Boom!

The Dead Meat Lice rule over all. What a walk-away. First the tower and then that far-out, far-off explosion. Dead Meat Lice rule over all.

Some explosions rip bodies by actually mashing them against air resistance. But if the body can move through the air resistance, then it becomes a missile in no more danger of destruction than a bullet—*if* it doesn't hit something.

When the car exploded, Remo was careful not to hit anything. He missed a stand of birch and kept fingernail, toenail tipping, like a spinner, a rudder, knowing that if something even as wide as a palm should touch surface, he would be grated against Route 8 like Parmesan cheese. It didn't and he wasn't.

But it was during that incredibly rapid spin that Remo for a few brief moments understood what sucking on a cloudstick meant. He forgot it, however, when the blood returned to his head.

The next morning, two messages reached the office of Dr. Harold W. Smith. One, from Remo, was that Vickie Stoner had been tagged and was waiting delivery to the Senate hearings. The other came from a clerk in Lucerne, Switzerland, who earned extra income by providing information.

He reported that a special bank account of a million dollars had been increased to $1.5 million. There were calls from all over the world about the account and there was a great mystery about it, but his educated guess was that the money was on deposit as payment for someone who could perform a specific task. Yes, he had heard of the last call. It had come from Africa, from a man named Lhasa Nilsson. He hoped the information might be of some value.

Nilsson. Nilsson. Smith had heard that name but where? He ran it through the giant computer complex at Folcroft, where hundreds of people fed it small packages of information, not really knowing what they were for, and only one outlet issued information, and that only to Smith.

Nothing. The computer was empty about Lhasa Nilsson. But Smith was still sure he recognized that name. There were two names in his memory. Lhasa Nilsson and Gunner Nilsson. He definitely had them associated with danger. But why? Why would he know it when the computer didn't? Smith watched a ketch tack across Long Island sound and casually watching the sails, this old form of sea transport, he suddenly remembered where he had heard about Nilsson.

He rang his secretary on the intercom.

Miss Stephanie Hazlitt knew Dr. Smith was somewhat peculiar, but all scientists had their foibles and what could one expect in a social research institute. But still, this was a little bit much. To be told mid-morning that Dr. Smith wanted an out-of-print adventure magazine which might be at an occult bookstore in Manhattan. He wanted it that day and if she felt she couldn't find it by phone, she should enlist the aid of the secretary of urban environment. Well, that was a bit much even for Dr. Smith. Too much.

Especially when she located by telephone a shop that had it and Dr. Smith told her to take a taxi both ways.

"To New York City and back, Dr. Smith?"

"Yes."

"That will cost sixty or seventy or maybe eighty dollars."

"Probably," Dr. Smith had said. When she got to the shop they wanted one hundred dollars for the magazine which had originally been priced at two cents. Of course, it was two cents in 1932 and there should be some markup, but five thousand times . . . well, that was too much. And the ride back to Folcroft was too much. And being stuck on the West Side Highway in traffic was too much, so to take her mind off it all, she read the magazine that was costing Folcroft almost two hundred dollars, not counting her day's salary. It was awful. Disgusting. Horrid.

The first article was about garrottes. It told how the most effective kind were made of materials that gave and that contrary to popular opinion, it was not Indian Thuggees who were best at it, but Romanians.

There was another article on Houdini which said his tricks were not really new but an adaptation of Japanese Ninja, copied from the most awesome assassins in ancient history, the Masters of Sinanju.

Well, who cared about that?

And then there was an article about a Swedish family. Perhaps that might prove more interesting, but in the entire article there was nothing about sex or even cooking.

There were only Count and Colonel Nilsson. The stories about them were enough to make one throw up. The most famous hunters of men alive, the family went back six hundred years to when Sweden was a military power. This one family had often served both sides in a war, selling their services to the highest bidder. They had killed a Polish prince by turning his bed into a pit of swords, and thought nothing, for a price, of clarifying the succession to a throne by removing competition.

A burgundian duke had hired them to kill a newborn baby who might in two decades have claim to Burgundy, but the child's father had also hired them to enhance his newborn son's chances. The baby was drowned in its bathwater. When the duke heard there was a similar price on his head, he attempted to buy off the Nilsson family. But the father of the dead child was so enraged that he kept raising his offer, until the duke could not match the sum. Knowing the cruelty of the Nilssons, the duke hanged himself.

Of course, the article stated, that was a long time ago and now neither Sweden nor the Nilssons were warlike. It was easy to believe looking at that lovely picture of the young Nilsson brothers in white shirts and shorts and blond hair, smiling from their ponies. Lhasa, nine, and Gunner, fifteen. Lhasa was going to be a singer and Gunner planned on medical research.

Well, that was the only nice thing in the entire magazine.

"Here's your trash," said Miss Hazlitt, giving Dr. Smith the magazine.

"You know, Miss Hazlitt, there is a funny

thing about computers. Information that goes in is called garbage in. And information that comes out is called garbage out. But nobody ever feeds it real garbage."

"Well, this magazine is certainly garbage, I'll tell you that."

"It certainly is, Miss Hazlitt. Thank you very much."

CHAPTER SEVEN

A water buffalo is stronger than a steer, but that is not what makes him more dangerous. A water buffalo will attack while dying, but that is not what makes him more dangerous. A water buffalo will attack when neither endangered nor hungry, but that is not what makes him more dangerous.

What makes a water buffalo more dangerous is that he likes to kill. And in that respect, he is like many men.

The African marsh ate at his clothes, but Lhasa Nilsson did not mind. His two bearers were huddled high in the crook of a tree, holding the only two guns of his expedition, but Lhasa Nilsson did not mind. His left foot tingled with the beginning of jungle rot, but Lhasa Nilsson did not mind. He had seen his water buffalo, dripping flowers from its mouth, chomping on the rich flora of the African equatorial marsh. His massive black shoulders and horns combined with a thick skull to make a physique that was mockery to all but the most powerful rifle, and then the rifle would have to shoot to perfection just to injure this creature.

Nilsson drew the arrow back to his cheek. The buffalo was forty yards upwind. If Nilsson had given this animal the advantage of smell, he would have been a dead man. But it was his genius, the genius of his family, that made advantage appear to be disadvantage. Why shoot for the skull when there was the whole body?

The buffalo lifted its head, listening. Nilsson released the arrow with a spitting swish of a sound. *Thwack,* the arrow drove into the flank of the buffalo. It snorted its anger, enraged but apparently uninjured.

A mere sting. The buffalo bellowed. To the horror of the gunbearers in the tree, the white man with the yellow hair lowered his bow and shouted:

"Buffalo, hah, hah, hah. Here I am."

The big black body, in almost arrogant joy, trotted the first few steps through the marsh, crushing plants and saplings. Then the hooves got steady footing and it lumbered into a charge, shaking the very tree in which the two gun bearers were cringing. The horns lowered and hooked but Lhasa Nilsson stood laughing, his hands on his hips. He looked up at the gun bearers in the tree and made a motion as if to shake it. One of the bearers shut his eyes and cried.

The buffalo was within fifteen paces when gray froth appeared at its mouth. It bellowed as its front legs stiffened, even while the body kept moving. The rear legs kicked as the beast boomed into the marshland, then fell and was still.

Lhasa Nilsson went to the dying buffalo. He

71

took its head in his hands, while straddling its sweaty black neck, and kissed the beast.

"Beautiful, beautiful animal. In you I see me, except I would know better than to charge when wounded by a poison arrow. It is the circulation that kills you when you are poisoned. I am sorry I never had the opportunity to teach you that. Good night, sweet beast, until we all meet in the sunrise fires."

Lhasa Nilsson clapped his hands, calling for the bearers. But they would not leave the tree. Did he not know that the water buffalo could spring to its feet with its last flicker of life and kill them all? Did he not understand the water buffalo?

Nilsson clapped his hands again. But the bearers would not come so he went back to his bow and strung it. Looking up at the tree, he aimed at a loincloth, which he saw was stained wet by fear.

"Do you know I can hit a target as small as a testicle with this?" he asked, and the bearers, clinging to the guns, scrambled down the tree. Nilsson gave the first bearer the bow and took the rifle.

"Now," he said, "where is the village that has the problem with a panther?"

It was another day's trek to the village. In the hot summer it was reduced to a collection of huts in a bowl of dust. They had too much water where they didn't need it, and too little where they did. But that was a mark of civilization, making over the environment to suit man. Funny how travelers would come to these places looking for wisdom. Here, wisdom was only being able to endure the consequences of one's own sloth, ignorance, and superstition.

Lhasa Nilsson ceremoniously greeted the head man.

"And how is your beloved brother, friend?" asked the head man, who stood as high as Nilsson's chest.

"As usual," said Nilsson glumly, and then, as an afterthought, "doing good works."

"He is a very good man. A blessed man," said the head man.

"Where is the panther?"

"That, we do not know. He is a giant among beasts, this panther. As big as the tigers. But where he is we do not know. He has killed a goat north of the village and attacked a man south of it and west his tracks have been spotted, but east is where he has killed a young woman and been seen many times."

"I see," said Nilsson. "You wouldn't know where and when he was seen, I take it." He stood with his arms crossed in the dusty little village, as men and women chattered away, trying to remember correctly on which day the black panther did what and where.

Nilsson knew he would not get a logical answer. He felt that probably the only creature worth anything in this entire valley was the panther. But Gunner had sent him up here and after all, Gunner was now the leader of the family, even if he didn't act like it. Lhasa was not about to break family tradition. Besides, with that phone call to Switzerland, he might yet convince Gunner that he was a Nilsson, even if the rest of the Swedes had forgotten they were Norsemen who took the Irish as slaves and looted the foul Anglo Saxons at will.

So Lhasa Nilsson who was fifty, but looked thirty, and felt the strength in his body of a youth of twenty, listened to the little brown man with disdain, trying not to show his true feelings lest Gunner get word that one of his precious little monkeys had been insulted.

"Thank you very much," said Lhasa, who received very little useful information. "You have been very helpful."

The head man offered Nilsson beaters, but Nilsson shook his head. He wanted to hunt leopard. Nilsson did not tell the head man that beaters turned the proud leopard into just another big frightened cat. He was tired of killing big frightened cats. He wanted that black panther on his terms, and on the panther's. Besides. The bearers were going to be a problem. They might tell Gunner about the buffalo, and Lhasa Nilsson would have to make sure they didn't do that.

So with his two bearers, he began his own hunt, by circling the village in ever-wider circles. He searched the way his family had taught him, not by looking at single twigs or branches, but by looking at the whole valley—seeing where the good drinking streams were, where the high ground was, where a black leopard might well seek a good prowl. He noticed that his bearers were nervous, so he made them walk in front of him. He came to the village where the woman had been slain. Her husband wept as he explained how he had gone to look for her and had found her remains.

"How many days ago?" asked Gunner. Lhasa.

But the man did not know. He sniveled that sunshine had been removed from his life.

"That is too bad," said Lhasa, who fought the urge to retch at this pathetic creature.

On the second day, Lhasa found fresh tracks.

74

The idiot bearers suggested it was a good place to clumb a tree and wait for the panther.

"This is where he has been, not where he is going," said Lhasa.

"But panthers often return on their tracks," the bearers said.

"This is not where he is going. I know where he is going. He is becoming annoyed with us and I know where he is going. In three minutes, we shall see an even fresher track."

They pushed on and almost within three minutes, one shouted out, pointing in astonishment to a wet track. Water was still oozing up into the paw print.

The bearers refused to proceed.

"Then this is the place you wish to stay?"

They both nodded.

"Then I shall go on alone." They followed as he knew they would. They who followed were being followed, he knew from that special almost-silence behind them that comes when a predator stalks. Birds sing differently and ground animals disappear.

"Would you like to climb your tree now?" asked Lhasa. The bearers, who had been stumbling over one another, couldn't agree fast enough. Lhasa told them to give him the guns and the long brush-cutting knives so they could climb better.

The first gripped the trunk with his legs and shinnied up a few feet; he was followed closely by the second. Lhasa gripped one of the bearer's guns by the barrel and swung it like an axe handle into the kneecap of the topmost man. Then with deft speed he positioned himself for the second man, as the first tumbled to the ground, screaming.

Thwack and Lhasa Nilsson got another man, another kneecap.

The first tried to crawl away, but Nilsson got the other kneecap and stomped the left wrist into shattered bone. The second lay on the ground, face forward, unable to move, his breath knocked out of him. With a savage kick, Lhasa shattered the man's left shoulder.

Naturally, if the men were found in this condition, it would be obvious that they had been beaten. But Lhasa knew he had an accomplice. The man with the broken wrist cried and begged Lhasa to spare his life.

"I will not take it," said Lhasa, "even if you beg me, and you will, you smelly little monkey."

Lhasa lit a cigarette, a gross foul-smelling local brand, and walked off into the jungle about thirty yards. The panther emitted his characteristic hiss and growl, and Lhasa heard the man scream, begging for quick release.

Well, he had promised he would not kill him, and he would not break his word. He heard the shrieks of terror, the growls, and then the chomping of bones. He wondered idly why chicken bones were dangerous for house cats but human bones didn't seem dangerous for the larger cats. Lhasa Nilsson finished the cigarette. He did not want to disturb the panther before the job was done. That wouldn't do. He checked the rifle again, quietly moving back the bolt. A copper-tipped beauty rested in the chamber.

Quietly, step by silent step, he made his way back toward the tree. With a sudden roar, the black panther, its open mouth still dripping blood, was launched in its leap at Nilsson. In the split second before he fired, Nilsson marvelled at the size and power of the beast. Surely the biggest panther he had ever seen. Then crack, thud, and the copper-tipped beauty went through the roof of the panther's mouth into the brain. Its charging body hurled Lhasa backward into a tangled vine, but he managed to block the claws with the stock of his rifle.

All in all, he was very relaxed, which was the only way to come out of one of these things alive.

He rolled out from beneath the leopard's heavy, twitching body. Its breath smelled like a sewer. He felt a numbing pain at his left shoulder. Why, the bugger had scored. His finger searched out the gash. Nothing too bad and it would look good for Gunner. Gunner would like that, especially since the bearers were dead. All in the love of his favorite little monkeys.

At the tree base, Lhasa saw the remnants of his bearers. Excellent. There would be no trace of a beating after that mauling. The bugger had been hungry indeed. Good thing. Sometimes, panthers wouldn't attack. Not like the beautiful water buffalo.

By the time Lhasa reached the hospital at what maps indicated as a town, the story had preceded him. It was just as he had told it at the village, just as the villagers had discovered the remains.

The village informed him that they would send the panther skin and two live pigs in thanks. Such was the generosity of Lhasa Nilsson that he announced to the natives that he would donate the skin to the widows of the bearers. "Let them sell it," he intoned. "I only wish I could have brought back their husbands."

He kept the pigs for himself. He liked fresh pork.

Dr. Gunner Nilsson was treating a child for

colic and lecturing the mother when Lhasa entered the office. Gunner was a half-inch taller and six years older, but he looked at least seventy. The lines were dug deep in his fine, tanned face, the pale blue eyes sad with many years of telling people that there was little he could do for them. His hospital was a hospital in name only. There were no operating rooms and the new antibiotics were for big cities and rich people. Gunner Nilsson could give only advice and some makeshift local remedies that, despite their mythic potency, had more power in the mind than in the bloodstream.

"I'm busy. Come back in a few minutes, please," said Gunner.

"I'm wounded," said Lhasa. "Even if I am your brother, I am wounded."

"Oh, I'm sorry. I'll look at it now." Gunner asked the woman with her child to come back in a few minutes. He did not wish to offend them, but he had a wounded man here.

Dr. Nilsson cauterized the wound because there was no antiseptic in the hospital powerful enough to cleanse it. He used a knife heated over coals. Lhasa made no sound, but when he was sure the smell of his burning flesh was in his brother's nostrils, he said:

"I understand now how difficult it must be for you to know that if you had the proper medicines, you could cure people instead of just watching them go off to die."

"What we do here, Lhasa, is better than nothing."

"It seems an injustice though, to offer less than we can. It seems an injustice that because of money people must die."

"What brings about this sudden sense of charity in you, Lhasa?" asked Gunner, wrapping the

78

shoulder in a cheap bandage expertly, so that the rough cloth allowed the wound room to breathe, yet prevented dirt from entering.

"Perhaps it is not charity, brother. Perhaps it is pride. I know what you can do, and to see a Nilsson fail day after day just for lack of money offends me."

"If you are suggesting that we revert to our traditional family work, find another suggestion, at least one that wasn't decided finally twenty-five years ago. How does the wound feel?"

"As well as sixteenth century medicine can make it."

"I am surprised the panther got that close to you. You never had that trouble before."

"I am getting old."

"You should have no trouble like this until you are in your seventies, considering what you know and what I have taught you."

"You saw the wound. You see all the wounds. All the infections, tumors, viruses, broken legs, and all the things you cannot help because you haven't supplies. I wonder what kind of supplies one million American dollars could buy. I wonder what kind of hospital that would build. How many natives could be trained in medicine for that much money."

"For all that much money, Lhasa, oh, the lives we could save. Drugs, doctors, medical technicians. I could make a million dollars into a hundred million dollars worth of healing." Dr. Nilsson returned the knife to the flames to cleanse it, because fire was the best antiseptic available in the primitive circumstances.

"How many lives could you save with that, brother?"

Dr. Gunner Nilsson thought a moment, then

shook his head. "I don't even want to entertain the thought. It makes me too sad."

"A hundred? A thousand?"

"Thousands. Tens of thousands," said Gunner. "Because the money could be used to create systems that would perpetuate themselves."

"I was wondering," said Lhasa. "If one person's life is worth thousands of native lives."

"Of course not."

"But she's white."

"You know how I feel about that. Too long has the color of a man's skin determined how long he will live."

"But she is rich and white."

"All the more reason," Gunner said.

Lhasa rose from his seat and tried to stretch the muscle of the cauterized wound. It throbbed as if it had its own heartbeat.

"There is a rich white woman in the United States whose very breath could give you the tools to help this land. But we are not in that business anymore so I must forget it. We are the last of the Nilssons. You settled that a long time ago."

"What are you talking about?" asked Gunner.

"The one million dollars is real, brother. I was not creating a hypothesis for you. I was giving you a plan of action."

"We will not use the family knowledge."

"Of course," said Lhasa, smiling. "I agree with you. And frankly I must confess I believe one rich white life to be worth much more than all the stinking natives of this stinking jungle."

"What are you doing to me?"

"I am allowing you, dear brother, to watch your patients die so that a rich white American can live. Of course, even that won't save her life because she will be dead shortly anyhow. But enjoy your ideals as you bury your little black friends."

"Get out of here," said Gunner. "Get out of my hospital."

But Lhasa left only the office. He waited in the ante room along with a woman whose gums were purple from chewing betel nut or from infection. Lhasa could not tell the difference, nor did he care very much.

In two minutes, Gunner strode from his private office.

"I'm here, brother," said Lhasa, laughing, and they left the hospital for a very long walk through the village.

Was Lhasa sure of the money?

Yes. He had heard of it four days ago when he was upriver. He had checked it out very carefully by telephone from the British staff officer's house. He still had some contacts on the continent. And he had finally talked to the man in charge of disbursing the money. It was firm. One and a half million dollars. The man had heard of the Nilsson family. He would be pleased if they would take the assignment.

"But when I returned you would not even speak to me but ordered me after this panther," Lhasa said.

"I have this fear, brother, that you like to kill for the sake of killing," Gunner said.

"Me, brother?"

"Of course you. Why did you take bow and arrow to hunt panther?"

"Did I do that?"

"You know you did. Were you hunting the buffalo again, an animal these villagers tame for their livelihood?"

"A buffalo likes to kill, brother," said Lhasa.

"Especially when you hunt it. I will tell you what I fear. I fear there is no money or little money in this thing and you just want to kill for enjoyment."

"Phone yourself, dear brother."

"I would have to teach you techniques, and I fear you would use them for your own pleasure."

"You taught me to hunt panther. Have I used that incorrectly?" Lhasa asked.

Dr. Gunner Nilsson paused near a mudhole on the main thoroughfare of the village. A young boy, his legs gnarled by a vitamin deficiency, hobbled along the dirt road.

"And, brother, why do you fear giving me knowledge which is rightfully mine? You know, it ends with me. I cannot pass it on to a son. And should I get about with this knowledge, practicing our family business, how many can I hurt compared with what poverty and ignorance does here?"

Twelve hours later, Lhasa Nilsson was upriver at the British field agent's telephone. He informed the man in Switzerland that he could deposit the money in an old Nilsson account. He had just learned of the account during an afternoon of intense discussion. Of that account and many things. He told the banker there would be no question of his collecting the money. And please keep other people out of the way. Amateurs only confused things.

CHAPTER EIGHT

When he was asked why eleven persons were killed and twenty-four injured at the North Adams Experience, the county sheriff replied that it was the result of close cooperation between all police departments.

"Thank God it wasn't the Beatles," he said, displaying his knowledge of contemporary music. "We really would have had a mess if they were here, although I think we could have done the same fine job."

The press agent for Maggot and the Dead Meat Lice did not have so easy an answer. He faced a problem. Should he say the Lice regretted what had happened or should he attempt to advertise it? The newspapers solved his problem for him.

Editorials railed against what they called the violent nature of acid rock. Stories compared the casualties at these concerts to guerilla wars. And a national television commentator asked, coast to coast, prime time: Does America Need This Abomination?

Shea Stadium in New York not only sold out for the Dead Meat Lice concert but the album, North Adams Experience, on which one could hear the bombs, sold 780,000 copies within ninety-six hours of the concert, not counting the bootleg editions produced in Mexico, Canada, and Bayonne, N.J.

What amazed Remo was how quickly the album was produced. When Vickie Stoner insisted she have one, Remo asked why, since she had heard much of it live.

"To live it again, man."

"You almost didn't live it the first time," Remo said.

"You the fuzz or something?" asked Vickie.

"No."

"Then why are you so heavy on my ass?"

"Because I want to see you alive."

"Why?"

"Because I love you, Vickie," said Remo, staring at her with the balanced power he had been taught and had found out was most effective with women.

"Okay, let's ball," said Vickie. Her tee shirt was over her head and flying across the hotel room by the time her blue jeans were unsnapped and falling around her ankles. She had young rising breasts with perfectly symmetrical ruby crests, firm smooth legs, and just a touch of softness around the hips.

She bounded backwards onto the bed, raising her legs in a V, her red hair fluffing over the pillow. The Waldorf Astoria in New York City had probably never seen such a fast disrobing in all its elegant history, thought Remo.

"What are you waiting for?"

"Stop playing hard to get," said Remo. "I mean, if you're going to make it an ordeal."

"C'mon already, I'm ready," said Vickie.

Remo went to the bed, wondering if even with all his powers he could have removed his slacks, tennis shirt, and loafers as quickly as his charge. He sat down beside her and placed a hand softly on her shoulder. He wanted to talk to her. There were problems and he had to explain that Chiun was not the sweet guru she thought he was, that one did not disturb the Master of Sinanju during his television shows and one never, absolutely never, touched one of his garments or tried to take something of his as a souvenir.

Remo squeezed her shoulder.

"Enough foreplay. Get to it," said Vickie.

"Vickie, I want to talk to you," said Remo. His hand moved to her breast.

"When you're ready, let me know," said Vickie. She squirmed out of bed. "I'm gonna ball the Master. I've waited long enough."

"Not now. He's watching his serials. No one ever disturbs Chiun when he's watching his soap operas."

"Until now."

"Until never," said Remo. He took her by one of her wrists that flailed at him, brought her back to the bed and, working her body to excitement, brought her to agonizing fulfillment. He tried to avoid falling asleep while doing it.

"Ooooh. Wow. What was that?" groaned Vickie.

"Balling," said Remo.

"It was never like that, not with anyone I've had. Where did you learn that? Wow. What a bitch. Rule over all. You're bitchen. Heavy. Heavy."

And she flipped her head back and forth against the pillow, tears of delight streaming from her eyes across her grace of freckles.

"Heavy, heavy."

Remo brought her to fulfillment two more times until, exhausted, she lay with her arms asprawl, her eyes half shut and a stupid little smile on her lips.

That should hold her for the afternoon, thought Remo, and wondered what she would do if he had really made love to her. It was an old truth that people on drugs only thought they made love better, like drunken drivers feeling very competent before meeting a ditch. Love making, however, was for the cool and the thoughtful and the competent, Remo knew. Even if it did take all the fun out of it.

Seven more days until she testifies, he thought, as he closed the door behind him and went to prowl the hotel, checking to see if anyone was moving in on them and Vickie.

Meanwhile, Vickie was thinking. If that straight could perform that well, imagine what the old gook could do? She had a point there. So, against the warnings of the straight with the short hair who knew how to ball like no one she had ever had, she opened the door to the adjoining room where the somebody was watching television. She heard one of the actors worry about Mrs. Cabot finding out that her daughter was hopelessly hooked on LSD, which was a gasser, man, because as Vickie knew, you didn't become an LSD junkie and besides what could a television show offer, compared to her fresh young body.

So between the somebody and the television she placed her crotch.

It came to pass that day that while the Master of Sinanju was taking his meager respite from the toils of the world, enjoying that one gracious artform flowering from the crude chaos that was white civilization, responding to the true beauty of delicate flowing drama, an apparition appeared before him. While Mrs. Cabot was exploring the gracious grief that was true concerned motherhood, an undressed girl did exhibit herself before the Master of Sinanju, as if there were some

86

special attraction to her vagina as opposed to all others.

Chiun removed it. Remo heard the thud down the hallway. He ran to Chiun's room and saw Vickie crumpled in the corner, her back against the wall, her pink duff pointed ceilingward, her head tucked against her chest, her breasts pressing against her cheeks.

"You killed her," yelled Remo. "You killed her. We're supposed to keep her alive and you killed her."

He skipped rapidly around Chiun, careful not to get between him and the picture, and listened to Vickie's heartbeat with his fingertips. Stopped. She was dead or in shock. He leveled her out on the floor and massaged the heart as Chiun had taught him. With his fingernails he created rapid movement in the hair as Chiun had taught him. The heart moved under Remo's ministrations, he released his hands slightly and her heart was beating by itself. He felt for broken bones, a rib that might have been sent into another vital organ. Chiun had taught that an opponent's rib is like a spear next to his heart, liver, and spleen.

The ribs were all right. His fingertips moved to the stomach and back, searching, as Sinanju was taught to search, to know the body through the hands. Then down to the soles of the feet and the toes. He had not fully learned this yet, but Chiun had taught that in the feet are all the nerves. One could, by manipulation of the toes, tell even if eyesight were failing. All Remo learned was that Vickie hadn't washed her feet.

"Heavy, man," groaned Vickie. Remo pressed his hands to her lips lest she further interrupt *As the Planet Revolves*.

And thus it came to pass that when the

Master of Sianaju had removed the obstruction of his modest pleasure, his student did further interrupt beauty with petty tantrums about incidents which may or may not have happened. Yet, under this assault against beauty, the Master of Sinanju did endure, for through the years, no matter how carefully he had tried to explain, his pupil had never learned to appreciate the one true beauty of his gross culture. It was not likely that he would learn now.

Chiun endured the sounds from the floor behind him. He endured the interruption of the girl, who said, "Heavy, man." He endured it all, for his heart was gentle enough and humble enough to endure almost anything.

And when the dramas for the day were over, he heard his ungrateful pupil rail against his pitiful attempt to enjoy a day, uninterrupted, of his beloved art.

"You could have called me. I would have gotten her out of your way. I would have removed her. You might have done what we're trying to prevent. Did you know that?"

Chiun did not answer, for how could one communicate with the insensitive? He would let his pupil vent his silliness, for Chiun's gentle heart could bear all outrages. Such was the purity of the spirit of the Master of Sinanju.

"Thank God there weren't any bones broken, but I don't know how, Chiun. She hit the wall like a catapult."

Why not? She had intruded like a . . . a . . . like a white man. But Chiun would not discuss that. There were some things one forgave one's pupil. There was one thing he could not forgive, however, and that was incompetence. On that he would speak.

"If your charge, that you were here to protect, was not with you, then why is your anger at me? It is not at me that your anger rails but at yourself for if you were properly discharging your duties, she could never have been here."

"I was clearing the rims as you taught me, Little Father, creating safety by going outward instead of staying inward."

"You cleared nothing if you left her alone to discover trouble. Where is she now?"

"She was able to walk and I put her in the other room so she wouldn't run afoul of you again while the shows were on."

"Then you are not with her?"

"Obviously."

"Then you are obviously a fool. This child has some good qualities I have not previously found in Americans. She understands the respect due a Master of Sinanju. You should have taught her about the American television treasures."

"I have a revelation for you, Little Father. She doesn't know Sinanju from the Assassins of Arabia, and she'd laugh at you if you tried to tell her about soap operas."

"The assassins were not of quality. Why would you compare the House of Sinanju to men who smoked their courage? And laugh? Why would anyone laugh at a Master of Sinanju?"

"You don't understand the counter culture in this country."

"How can one have a counter to something that does not exist? Truly puzzling. But what is not puzzling is your incompetence. I have told you what you must do, but you do not do it. You prefer to argue and fail than to listen and succeed. Such is the case with many people, but never before with a pupil of the House of Sinanju."

So with scarcely a "yes, Little Father," Remo went into the other room and Vickie Stoner was gone. He checked the bathroom and the hall. He went to the stairwells and listened. He ran to the lobby. But Vickie Stoner was not there. Just a small commotion at the registration desk. A Swedish man with a very deep tan, as if he had lived in the sun for thirty years, was arguing with the clerk and with three blacks in black, red, and green skullcaps.

"My name is Nilsson and I expressly made a reservation for today. You must have it. Lhasa Nilsson."

CHAPTER NINE

Abdul Hareem Barenga, alias Tyrone Jackson, didn't give the bellboy a tip because he was a lacky of imperialism, an Uncle Tom and an Oreo. These were the real reasons.

The incidental reason why was that these white mu-fus at the registration desk downstairs had demanded the room fee in advance which had taken the last of the money from St. Louis.

"We outa juice, baby?" asked Philander Jones, looking around the Waldorf Astoria Hotel room, which he figured he could clean out and resell for at least $1,300, if he could get everything past the doorman.

"We not outa juice," said Barenga. "We beginning to capitalize the revolution."

"We shoulda waited for the welfare before we begun the revolution 'cause that's two hundred right there."

"The revolution don't need no welfare. It need capitalization. And we gettin' it."

"Two hundred is two hundred."

"You think like a nigger, you always gonna be a nigger, nigger. We listen to you, we do this job for seven, maybe eight hundred. You think capitalization and you know what the man is doing. Gotta think like the man to beat the man."

Philander Jones had to admit that Barenga was right again. When that Guinea mafioso had been buried in that closed coffin and the money had come out of the wreath and then that candyman Sweet Harold had told them about all that bread on an open contract, Barenga had played it real cool, man. Went right to that white guinea trucking outfit, sitting in the main office like he owned it and had put the man down and down and down.

"I don't need no white mu-fu tell me how to do a mu-fu job," Barenga had said, sitting with his feet right up there on that guinea's desk and the guinea not saying nothing. Nothing.

"You should see her picture first. To get the right one."

"Ah ain't here 'cause I love you, honkey. I ain't here 'cause I think you anything but a pale dead meat copy of the original man. Capital. I'm here for capital. My army needs capital. You wanna deal, honkey, you deal capital."

"How much capital?" asked the vice president of Scatucci Trucking.

"Twenty thousand big ones."

"That would be two thousand dollars, right?"

"Yo ears fulla shit, honkey. I said big ones. Twenty thousand dollars."

"That's a lot of money," said the vice president of the trucking firm. "You drive a hard bargain. I'll give you four hundred now and the rest when the job is done."

"You ain't dealing with no jive-ass nigger, honkey. Now break out some of that good scotch you keep around for business deals. And keep your lips off the bottle."

Barenga and Philander had finished the bottle of Johnny Walker Black in the truck terminal and then they went to the HiLo, where they had scotch and cola, scotch and Seven Up, scotch and Snow White, and scotch and Kool Aid, all from the top of the shelf—Black Label, Chivas Regal, Cutty Sark. The Chivas and the Snow White was the best. By morning, the four-hundred dollars up front was exhausted and when they went back to the trucking terminal for more money, the honkey wasn't there, but Sweet Harold pulled up in his hog, a white Eldorado and he said their asses would be in New York City by that afternoon or their asses wouldn't be at all. He showed them the photograph of the white fox with the red hair and said she was the hit and they'd better make a good try or Sweet Harold would cut them up for good.

"We expended the capital," Barenga tried to explain. "Man, a good hit costs money."

"You drank it up at the HiLo," said Sweet Harold.

"We had a taste at the HiLo," said Barenga.

"You were buying everyone at the HiLo and then you blew the rest on two foxes, Tyrone. You shouldn't have done that, Tyrone. That is a very nice way to get killed, do you hear me, Nigger Tyrone?"

"We can't get to New York without bread, man. Even if you gonna waste us."

"You have damaged my reputation, Tyrone. I told the man you were good and you go drinking up your carfare like some field nigger, Tyrone. That is not nice, is it, Tyrone?"

"No. Ain't nice."

"Is it, Philander?"

"No. Ain't nice."

"Is it, Piggy?"

"No. Ain't nice."

"Now it just so happens that the bread you spent was on my foxes and it just so happens that I am going to lend you some money and three tickets to New York City. Now I have been informed that your hit was seen in the Waldorf Astoria so you will check in there. If you are not checked in there before dinner today, I will hunt your ass good. Do you understand, Tyrone?"

"Dig it, man."

"All right, Barenga. Unleash your Black Army of Liberation."

"That fox is already dead meat, brother," said Barenga. "You gonna take us to the airport?"

"If I see you touch one of my beautiful leather seats with your scruffy ass, nigger, I will peel the skin from your head."

It was decided as Barenga went to his sister's home to change into some good threads for New York that after the revolution they would not even try to make Sweet Harold into a new man. He would be wasted along with the honkeys.

Barenga's sister eyed him suspiciously. "I been hearing some weird things about you three. You picking up a contract nobody else gonna touch."

Barenga told his sister that the Black Army of Liberation of Free Africa did not divulge strategy.

"Ain't nobody touching that contract," yelled his sister. "You think if it was any good Sweet Harold wouldn't do it hisself? Do you think the guineas would give it to Sweet Harold if they thought they could deliver themselves? Do you know you getting nothing and Sweet Harold and the guineas are getting the bread? Everybody know that but you, Tyrone. Sweet Harold get five thousand dollars just for delivering your ass to the man. He gonna get a quarter of a million dollars if you make the hit, and what're you gonna get? Everyone laughing at you three."

Abdul Hareem Barenga smacked his sister into the door. On the plane he explained to Philander and Piggy that nothing his sister said was true. It was just the black woman's fear of the black man assuming his role as king that had gotten to her. He had hit her to teach her her place.

"That's right. She gettin' uppity," said Piggy. And Philander agreed because Barenga sure did a putdown on that guinea honkey at the truck terminal. They all laughed at that and decided that after the revolution they might let some honkeys live, like the stewardess with the nice ass.

When they got to the Waldorf and that foreign guy with the real white-yellow hair had tried to get in front of them, didn't even know how to make a line, why Barenga had put this whole jive hotel in its place. And it had worked. He got served first, while that foreign honkey just stepped back and took it, smiling.

"This the new field headquarters of the Black Army of Liberation," announced Barenga. "We gonna plan our strategy and tactics."

"As field marshal," said Philander, "I suggest we provision the troops."

"As Major general, I agree," said Piggy.

"As your supreme commander in chief. I will follow the will of my army," said Abdul Hareem Barenga and he phoned room service and ordered three of them big steaks and three bottles of Chivas Regal, and what did the Waldorf mean it didn't have any Snow White soda pop? Well, how about Kool-Aid? Okay, any fruit drink? Did he want filet mignon? No, he did not. He wanted steaks. Big ones. And it better be choice meat. He didn't want to feed his army gristle.

Shortly after he ordered, a knock sounded at the door.

"When the man see the Black Army, he move," said Philander.

Barenga chuckled as Piggy opened the door. The foreign honkey with the white-yellow hair stood in the door, smiling. He wore a purple lounging jacket, soft gray slacks, and slippers.

"I hope I'm not intruding," he said in that funny voice.

"I don't give a shit what you hope. Don't bother with us," said Barenga.

"I couldn't help overhearing you talk to the clerk," he said.

"Well, then, you just stop up your ears iffen you can't help none," said Barenga; Piggy and Philander laughed.

"When you asked which room Vickie Stoner was in, I thought that was rather gross. As a matter of fact, I found it incredible that anyone would be stupid enough to publicly ask where to reach his victim. Incredibly stupid."

"You want to get your ass busted, honkey?" said Barenga.

"I don't know if your little monkey brain can absorb this, but when you publicly announce you are on a hunt, then you become the hunted."

"What you jivin', man? Get outta here."

Lhasa Nilsson sighed. He looked down the hallway right, he looked down the hallway left, and having made sure no one could see him, took a little automatic pistol from the pocket of his lounging jacket and put a copper-tipped .25 caliber bullet between the left and right eyes of a black man whose nickname he never bothered to find out was Piggy. The shot made a soft, hardly noticeable crack, like a dish breaking over a sofa. Piggy's head jerked slightly and he collapsed right where he had been standing.

Nilsson stepped into the room and kicked the door closed.

"Get him under the bed," ordered Nilsson.

Philander and Barenga couldn't grasp what had happened. They stared dumbly at Piggy, who looked as if he were sleeping on the floor except for a little fountain of blood bubbling from the bridge of his nose.

"Move him under the bed," said Nilsson again, and Barenga and Philander suddenly understood what had happened. They stuffed Piggy under the bed, avoiding each other's eyes.

"There's a bloodstain there," said Nilsson, nodding toward the spot where Piggy had fallen. "Clean it up."

Philander rose to get a cloth, but Nilsson nodded to the supreme commander of the Black Liberation Army of Free Africa. "No. You. What's your name?"

"Abdul Kareem Barenga."

"What kind of name is that?"

"Afro-Arab," Barenga said.

"It is neither African nor Arab. Put some water on the cloth. Now this is what you're going to do. While I was waiting in the hall I heard you order food. You are going to tip the waiter very well. You are going to tip him ten dollars and then you will hold another hundred in your hand while you say you are looking for a white girl whom you will describe. You will not say Vickie Stoner, but you will describe the red hair and the freckles, and will say that she is someone you fancy and came to New York to find. You will not let the waiter in the room, but you ... what's your name?"

"Philander."

"You, Philander, will take the tray and hold the door. Take the tray with your left hand and hold the door open with your right. You will allow the waiter to partially enter, but not beyond the open door. I will stand behind it with this little weapon here, which is more than sufficient for both of you and the waiter should that be necessary. Do you understand?"

"What if the waiter don't know where she is?"

"Waiters, cooks, liverymen, butlers, gardeners, keepers of the chamber, keepers of the gate, know these things. They are traditionally the breach in the walls of every castle. It is an old family saying of ours ... breach in the wall of a castle? I see you don't know what that is. Well, a long time ago people defended themselves by living in stone houses that were actually forts. A fort is a place designed to be safe from attack, hard to get into."

"Like a bank, or them new liquor stores," said Philander.

"Right," said Nilsson. "And we discovered a long time ago that servants were a breach in this

97

wall, meaning an opening. As if someone left the door to the liquor store open at night."

"Dig, baby," said Barenga. "That's strategy. Like the great black Hannibal."

"The what Hannibal?"

"Hannibal, black. He African. Greatest general what ever generalled."

"I don't know why I'm bothering," said Nilsson. "But we apparently have some time. First, Hannibal was a great general but not the greatest. He lost to Scipio Africanus."

"Another African," said Barenga, smiling.

"No, he got the name Africanus after defeating Hannibal at the battle of Zama in North Africa. Scipio was Roman."

"The guineas got him?" asked Barenga in astonishment.

"Yes. In a way."

"They done in black Hannibal?"

"He wasn't black," said Nilsson. "He was Carthaginian. That's now North Africa. But the Carthaginians were Phoenicians. They came from Phoenicia ... what would now be Lebanon. He was white. A semite."

"Them Semites ain't black?"

"No. Never were. Still aren't, except those who have bred with blacks."

"But Hannibal black, real black. I seen it on TV. The Afro-Sheen hair commercial. Hannibal even got corn rows. Now, no white man got corn row hair."

"Just because it's on television doesn't make it so."

"I seen it. I seen it with my own eyes. He got this boss gold helmet with feathers and corn row hair."

"I give up," said Nilsson. "Do you have money for the waiter?"

"I don't tip no . . ." Barenga saw the nasty little barrel level at his head. "Got no bread, man."

Nilsson's left hand skillfully went to a pocket without disturbing his concentration on his gun. He threw some new American money on the bed. "Remember now. Ten dollars tip. Keep him just the other side of the door. You fancy this red-headed girl with freckles. You hold the hundred dollars up. And take off that stupid little beanie. No one is going to believe you'd throw away a hundred to find a woman, not with that silly little thing on your head."

"Them my Afro colors," said Barenga.

"Put it away."

There were three raps at the door. "Room service."

The beanie disappeared behind Barenga on the bed.

"Come in," said Barenga. He smiled nervously at the little gun.

Philander opened the door with his right hand and with his left wheeled a two-layered stainless steel cart, draped with white cloth, into the room. Barenga rose from the bed and went to the door.

The waiter was a round jello-soft little man with a cherub's pink face. He opted for liberalism and racial consciousness the instant he saw the ten-dollar bill in Barenga's hand. As he pocketed it, he said "Thank you, sir," although only three minutes before he had told the room service captain that he would probably wrap the food trays around those niggers' heads.

Barenga pushed the tray into the room behind him but still stood in the open door. Before the waiter could turn to go, Barenga held the hundred-dollar bill in his right hand, waving it slowly like someone teasing a house cat with an old slipper.

The waiter saw the bill and stopped. He could see the light green and the dark green ink on the creamy colored paper. He saw the extra zeroes in the corner of the bill. He decided that liberalism was too weak a posture to adopt in the latter third of the twentieth century. He would become an advocate of radical power.

"Yes, sir," he said, his watery blue eyes meeting Barenga's. "Will there be anything else, sir?" He looked again at the bill in Barenga's hand.

Barenga was wondering how he and Philander could keep the hundred. It would be a good start on capitalizing the revolution. He saw the movement of Nilsson's sleeve behind the door and decided the revolution would have to wait.

"Yeah, man," Barenga said. "You know the people in this hotel?"

"Yes, sir. I think so."

"Well, I'm looking for a special one. This one is a little red-haired honkey with freckles."

"A girl, sir?" the waiter said, telling himself that distaste and revulsion were unworthy emotions for a radical to feel, just because a black man asked about a white woman.

"Well, of all the sheeit," said Barenga. "Yeah, a girl. I look like I like boys?" He waggled the hundred-dollar bill at the waiter.

"There is such a young lady," the waiter said.

"Ummm?"

The waiter said nothing else, so Barenga said, "Well, where is she?"

The waiter looked at the hundred-dollar bill again and without taking his eyes off it, said, "She is in Room 1821. That's on the eighteenth floor. She is with an elderly gentleman of the Oriental persuasion and another young man."

"He a dink too?"

"A dink?"

"Yeah. A gook. A Jap."

"No, sir. He is an American."

Barenga had decided. That hundred dollars was just too much to pay for such horseshit information. He curled it back into his hand and stuffed it into the slit pocket of his dashiki.

"Thanks, man," he said, backed up and quickly closed the door on the startled waiter.

He turned to Nilsson with a small happy smile.

"How'd I do?"

"Fine, until you stole that hundred dollars from the waiter," Lhasa said.

In the hallway, the waiter was staring at the closed door and reaching the same conclusion. One hundred dollars was a lot of money. It could buy 50 sheets or maybe enough wood for 10 crosses to burn on someone's lawn, or hundreds of feet of heavy rope for lynchings.

Barenga moved back warily as Lhasa came from behind the door. "Give me back the hundred," Nilsson said. The gun was still aimed at Barenga, its evil black hole seeming to stare at him in black dark hatred.

Lhasa smiled.

The door swung open behind him. "Listen here, you fucking blootch," the waiter shouted as he barged into the room. "You owe me."

The swinging door hit Lhasa Nilsson in the middle of the back and he was propelled forward a few steps toward the bed on which Philander sat. He pulled himself up short, turned to the waiter, who had stopped, speechless, inside the doorway, and squeezed the trigger of the small .25 caliber revolver. A hole opened in the waiter's throat like a red flower opening to greet the sunshine. The waiter's eyes widened. His mouth worked as if he were going to talk, to impart one last piece of wisdom. Then he fell forward onto the rug.

Nilsson moved forward quickly and kicked the door shut. "Get him under the bed," he snarled. Barenga moved quickly, hoisting the pudgy waiter by the armpits. "Philander, you help me," he said, his voice dripping hurt.

Philander hopped up from the bed and grabbed the dead waiter's feet.

"Man, you didn't have to do that," Philander complained to Lhasa Nilsson.

"Shut up," Nilsson said. "We're going to have to hurry now. The waiter will be missed. Take off his jacket before you put him away."

Barenga began to open the buttons.

"Tell me," said Nilsson, "do you wear any trousers under that ridiculous sheet you parade around in?"

Barenga shook his head.

"All right, then, take off his pants too."

Barenga and Philander stripped the waiter and finally Barenga stood up with jacket and trousers over his arm. Philander rolled the waiter's body under the bed and straightened out the bedspread so it was neat again and would discourage anyone from a random look under the bed.

"Which of you wants to play waiter?" asked Nilsson.

Barenga looked at Philander. Philander looked at him. No one spoke. Being asked to be a waiter was as bad as being asked to tap dance on a watermelon rind.

"One of you has to wheel this cart of food up to Room 1821. Now which one'll do it?"

Barenga looked at Philander. Philander looked at him.

As Barenga looked at Philander, he heard that frightful click again and it froze him in his position. And then the hissing thwap of a shot, and then the first spurt of blood out of Philander's left temple, before Philander dropped to the floor.

"I think he was too stupid to pass for a waiter," Nilsson said as Barenga turned toward him. "Now you put on the uniform and do it fast. We don't have much time."

Barenga decided he would take no more time than was absolutely necessary, thus proving to Nilsson his loyalty and absolute trustworthiness. In twenty-two seconds he had peeled off the dashiki and put on the uniform jacket and pants.

Nilsson finished rolling Philander under the overcrowded bed and turned to inspect Barenga.

"I believe most waiters wear shirts," he said. "I've never seen one before wearing a jacket over his bare skin."

"I ain't got no shirt," Barenga said. "But if you want, I'll look for one," he added hurriedly.

Nilsson shook his head. "Never mind," he said. "The sight of the jacket should do all right. Let's go."

They rode up in an empty service elevator. At the eighteenth floor, Nilsson stepped out and looked both ways before motioning Barenga to follow him.

Barenga moved out slowly onto the carpeted floor and began to wheel the car along the hallway, a respectful three paces behind Nilsson. He was a cold mu-fu, this blond, kinky honkey. Barenga was going to keep an eye on him. He didn't act right. He was too quick to pull that trigger. Man, like he was dedicated. He had that look in his eyes like one of those social workers, man, that was always going to do everything and fix everything and make everything right, man, 'cause they had all that love, you know, love. They were so goddamn sure of themselves, man, they was like dedicated, like the minister of the Abyssinian Church, and then at knifepoint, you asked one of them for a penny, and suddenly, they realized everything wasn't going to be as easy as they thought. At least the smart ones learned that. The stupid ones, who were more numerous, never learned nothing. But this cat was funny like, because he knew plenty, but he still had that dedicated look.

Barenga stopped pushing the cart and stepped forward to Nilsson, who had beckoned him with a crooked finger. "Now you knock on the door and when you get an answer, tell them Room Service. When the door opens, I'll handle everything else. You got that?"

Barenga nodded.

CHAPTER TEN

Only a few feet away, another man nodded.

Separated from Nilsson and Barenga by the wall of the apartment, Chiun pressed a button, turning off the last of his favorite afternoon television shows. He settled back into full Lotus position and allowed his eyes to close.

Remo, he knew, had gone to look for the intrusive wench. He would no doubt find her; that she could vanish was really too much to be hoped for. That would be simple and in America life was never simple.

It was a very strange country, he mused, as his eyes closed gently. Chiun had worked for too many emperors to believe in the superiority of the masses, but in America the masses were right. Everyone could live in happiness if only people would respect everyone else's right to be left alone. That was all the masses wanted in America, to be left alone. It was the one thing they never got, he reflected. Instead, they got social tinkering, and the tensions and troubles that tinkering caused.

How unlike Sinanju, the tiny village that Chiun was from but had not seen in years. Yes, it was poor by American standards but the people were rich in many ways. Each lived his own life and did not try to live another's. And the poor, the aged, the weak, and the children, they were cared for. It did not require social programs, politicians' promises, and long speeches, just the income from the skills of the Master of Sinanju. For over a thousand years the village had hired out its Master as an assassin, and his labors supported those in the village who could not support themselves.

This was Chiun's responsibility. As he sat with his eyes closed, his mind on the edge of sleep, he thought it had been just and fair, a rich and honest life. The Master of Sinanju had always performed his missions, and the emperors he had served had always paid. Now his "emperor" was Dr. Smith, the head of CURE and Remo's employer. Dr. Smith also paid.

Why could America not handle its social

problems in the same efficient way it handled its need for assassins and their skills? But that would be simple, and simplicity was not the white man's way. It was not their fault; just that they had been born defective.

Chiun heard the knock on the door but decided not to answer it. If it was Remo, he could get in. Anyone else would be looking for Remo or the girl, and since neither of them were here, there was no point in opening the door to say that when a closed unanswered door could deliver the same message.

Rap! Rap! Rap! The knocking was louder now. Chiun ignored it more, if that were possible.

"Hey. This here is Room Service," a voice brayed from the hallway. *Rap! Rap! Rap!*

If the man hammered on the door long enough he would eventually get tired, perhaps so tired that for sustenance he might eat the food he was carrying. That would be punishment enough. Chiun dozed.

In the hallway, Lhasa Nilsson put a hand on the doorknob and turned it. The door opened noiselessly.

"No one here," he said. "Bring the cart and we'll wait."

"Why bring the cart?"

"Because it gives us a reason to be inside. Bring the cart."

Chiun had heard the door open, had heard the voices, and as Nilsson and Barenga entered the apartment, he rose and turned to face the two men.

Nilsson saw the last part of Chiun's fluid rise from the floor and the way he turned. Something he recognized in it made him move his hand close to his jacket pocket, where he kept the small revolver.

"Hey, old man, why don't you answer the door?" Barenga growled.

"Quiet," Nilsson commanded. Then to Chiun, he said, "Where is she?"

"She has gone," Chiun said. "Perhaps to join the circus?" He folded his hands in front of his light green robe.

Nilsson nodded; he watched Chiun's hands move, slowly, without threat, carefully.

"Check the rooms," he told Barenga. "Look under the beds."

Barenga headed for the first bedroom while Nilsson returned his eyes to Chiun.

"Of course, we know each other," Nilsson said.

Chiun nodded. "I know of you," he said. "I do not think you know me."

"But we are in the same trade?" Nilsson said.

"Profession," Chiun said. "I am not a shoemaker."

"All right, profession," Nilsson said with a small smile. "Are you here to kill the girl too?"

"I am here to save her."

"Too bad," Nilsson said. "You lose."

"There is a time for everything under the sun," Chiun said.

Barenga came out of the bedroom. "That one's empty," he announced, and went to the next bedroom.

"It is good you have such efficient, intelligent help," Chiun said. "A young house like yours needs assistance."

"A young house?" Nilsson said. "The Nilsson name has been famous for six hundred years."

"So too was that of Charlemagne and other blunderers."

"And who are you to be so officious?" Nilsson asked.

"It is unfortunate that you are so obviously the youngest of your family. Your elders would not need to ask the identity of the Master of Sinanju."

"Sinanju? You?"

Chiun nodded and Nilsson laughed.

"I can't understand your arrogance," Nilsson said. "Not after what my family did to your house at Islamabad."

"Yes, you are the youngest," said Chiun. "Because you have learned no lessons from history."

"I know enough history to know that the army we supported defeated the army you supported," Nilsson said. "And you know it too."

"Masters of Sinanju are not foot soldiers," Chiun said. "We were not there to win the war. Tell me, what happened to the pretender you put onto the throne?"

"He was killed," Nilsson said slowly.

"And his successor?"

"Killed, too."

"And did your history lessons teach you who then assumed the throne?"

Nilsson paused. "The man we deposed."

"That is correct," Chiun said. "And yet you say the House of Sinanju was defeated? By an upstart family only six hundred years old?" He laughed aloud, a high piercing cackle. "We should always lose thus. We were to protect the emperor and maintain his throne. A year later when we left, he was still alive, his throne still secure. His two enemies had met sudden death." Chiun extended his arms to his sides as if administering a blessing. "Pride is a good thing for a house to have, but it is

108

dangerous for its individual members. They stop thinking and live on pride instead, and he who lives on pride does not live long. As you will learn."

Nilsson smiled. His right hand came away slowly from his pocket, holding the automatic revolver.

Barenga reentered the room. "Whole place empty," he said.

"Fine," Nilsson said, his eyes not moving from Chiun's. "Sit down and be quiet. Tell me, old man, how did you know me?"

"The House of Sinanju never forgets those it has fought. Each master is taught their motions, their characteristics. Your family, for instance. As it was with your forebears, it is with you. Before you move, you blink your eyes hard. Before you put your hand to your pocket, you clear your throat."

"Why learn that?" Nilsson asked. "What good can it do you?" He now aimed the pistol squarely at Chiun's chest, across the eight feet of living-room carpet that separated them.

"You know that," Chiun said. "Why ask?"

"All right. It's to learn your enemy's weaknesses. But then why tell the enemy?"

Barenga sat against the wall, watching the conversation, his head swiveling, as if he were watching a tennis match.

"One tells the enemy to destroy him. As with you. Even now, you worry about your ability to pull that trigger without blinking your eyes. That worry will destroy you."

"You are very sure of yourself, old man," Nilsson said, a slight smile playing at his face. "Is that not the kind of pride you said could destroy a man?"

Chiun straightened to his full height. He still was a head shorter than Lhasa Nilsson. "For anyone else, perhaps," he said, "but I am the Master of Sinanju. Not a member of the Nilsson family." His contempt, crisp and unmistakable, triggered fury in Nilsson.

"That is your hardship, old man," he said. His finger tightened on the trigger. He tried to concentrate on Chiun who still stood, unmoving, in the center of the floor. But his eyes. What would his eyes do? Nilsson felt the first nudge of doubt creep into his brain. He tried to block it out, but could not. So he squeezed the trigger, but as he did, he realized he had blinked. Both eyes had shut tightly, an ancestral curse handed down through the ages. He did not have to see to tell his bullet missed. He could hear it chip off the plaster wall. He did not have to be told that he would never get another chance to fire. Suddenly, he felt the pain in his stomach and felt his body drifting away. All because of a blink. If only he could warn Gunner.

Before he died, Lhasa Nilsson gasped, "You are lucky, old man. But someone else will be coming. Someone better than I."

"I shall greet him with kindness and respect," Chiun said. Those were the last words Lhasa Nilsson ever heard.

Those were the last words that Abdul Kareem Barenga ever wanted to hear. "Feet, get moving," he yelled, and, wailing like a flute at midnight, he ran to the front door of the apartment, yanked it open and raced off down the hallway.

Remo had been worried. He had found no trace of Vickie Stoner. No one had seen her, no cabbie, bellhop, policeman, no one. Already he and Chiun had mucked it up, and right at the moment, he had no idea where to look. The girl had been so spaced out while Remo had been with her that he could not recall anything she might have said that offered a clue to where she might go.

Losing the girl made him angry; not knowing where to look for her made him more angry. Neither factor really had anything to do with Abdul Kareem Barenga, but it was Barenga's bad luck to be the unfortunate vessel that received Remo's displeasure.

When the elevator door opened on the eighteenth floor, Remo stepped out and was overrun by Barenga, who charged the elevator as if leading his Black Liberation Army of Free Africa to free samples at the welfare office.

"Calm down," Remo said. "What's the hurry?"

"Honkey, move on over," said Barenga, who had occupied his time waiting for the elevator to arrive by clawing at the closed elevator door. "I gotta get out of here." He tried to push Remo from the empty elevator.

Fully annoyed now, Remo grabbed the elevator door with one hand and refused to move. Barenga pushed, but he might as well have been pushing at the base of the Empire State Building.

"What's the hurry, I said?"

"Man, you get out of here. There's a crazy yellow man back there gonna kill us all, you not careful. Man, I gotta get me a cop."

"Why?" Remo said, suddenly cautious, wondering if Chiun's television shows had run late this day.

" 'Cause he just killed a man. Oooweee. He just hop across that room and he move that foot like magic and that man die. He just up and die.

111

Ooooweee. Too many people getting killed today. I gotta get me a cop."

His eyes rolled wildly in his head and Remo saw that Barenga would not settle for just a cop. A cop, a hundred cops, the state police, the sheriff's office, the U.S. Attorney, the FBI and the CIA. If they all came in now to protect Barenga, wearing full battle dress and marching in close order, he would still be in a state of panic. Remo needed no more complications this day. Nothing resolved complications faster than death.

"You do that," Remo said. "You go get a cop. Tell them Remo sent you." He stepped back out of the doorway and as Barenga reached forward to tap a button,. Remo drove a hard right index finger into the black man's clavicle. By the time Barenga hit the floor, Remo was humming, busily working on the elevator control panel. He found the electrical cable cutoffs and shredded the wires with his fingers, so that nothing would work on the elevator, except the force of gravity. He backed out of the car, reached in through the open door, and tapped two wires together, then jumped back. The elevator unlocked itself and started down with an intensifying *whoosh*. Remo looked through the still-open door, down the shaft, as the elevator picked up speed on its way to the subbasement.

He could feel warm air circulating around the back of his neck in the wake of the runaway elevator. He continued to watch until he saw and felt the elevator crash at the bottom of the shaft. Its walls crumpled as if made of typing paper. Cables slithered down and fell on top of the car. Heavy clouds of greasy dust coughed up.

Remo stepped back, rubbing his hands briskly. He felt better now. Nothing like a little tussle with an intellectual problem to clear the troubled mind.

He felt so good that he was able to ignore Chiun's rantings about an upstart offspring of an upstart house insulting the Master of Sinanju. Remo just quietly shoved Lhasa Nilsson's body into a closet for safekeeping until he could figure out a way to shame Chiun into disposing of it.

CHAPTER ELEVEN

Big Bang Benton hit the button that activated his recorded theme music, waited for the engineer's gesture that signaled that his microphone was dead and he was off the air, then stood up and waved to the twenty-five girls who were observing his small studio from behind protective soundproofed glass.

He rubbed a hand over his head, careful not to mess up the expensive woven hair piece, stretched himself luxuriously, then motioned again. The girls responded with cheers and eager waving of their own.

Benton stepped forward toward the glass, an awkward, pear-shaped man, thumping heavily on the heels of his blue Cuban boots. As if on signal the girls, most of them in their early teens, ran forward. They pressed their faces against the glass like hungry urchins on Thanksgiving, and Benton could hear their squeals when he ran his fingers through his hair again. He lowered the almost-black smoked glasses he wore until they perched on the end of his nose, and he leaned his face forward to the glass, careful not to press his body against it because it might crush the rolled satin flowers on his purple and white satin shirt.

He mouthed the words against the glass.

"Who wants to come in and talk with the old Banger?"

He heard the usual shriek go up and leaned back to examine the reaction. Twenty-five girls. Twenty-five takers. Wait. Twenty-four.

The one who wasn't taking was a freckle-faced redhead with a sleek, lithe body and a face man, that was zonkier than zonked.

She had to be high, because she looked bored, and young girls did not get bored in the presence of Big Bang Benton.

Big Bang fixed her with his never-fail stare over the dark glasses, letting his eyes sing her songs of love and lechery waiting just around the corner.

The girl yawned. She didn't even bother to cover her mouth with her hand.

That decided Big Bang. He waved to a young pimply-faced usher who stood behind the crowd of girls, and then pointed to the redhead. Without another word, he turned away, left his studio and headed down the hallway to his dressing room. A dressing room was totally useless for a disc jockey, who could work in his underwear. But Big Bang Benton, who had been hooked on show business since he was Bennet Rappelyea of Batavia, New York, fifteen years earlier, had insisted upon and gotten one in his new contract.

Damn good thing too, he thought. Because if the station had balked about it, Big Bang was prepared to leave and take his following to any of the other dozen stations in the city that were falling all over themselves to sign him. When the Banger whistled, the station danced, and for the frustrated entertainer, there was a kind of sweet music in that too.

Back inside the studio, the teeny boppers were making less than sweet music.

"Who does he think he is, walking away like that?" one demanded.

"But he smiled at us. Maybe he'll be back," said her companion.

The usher approached the redhead.

"Big Bang wants to see you," he said, touching the girl's arm.

She turned and looked deep into his pimples, her eyes not quite focused.

"Does he really know Maggot?" she asked, her voice mushy thick, as if her tongue tip were stuck to the back of her lower teeth.

"The Banger knows everybody, honey. They're all his friends," the usher said.

"Good," said Vickie Stoner. "Gotta ball that Maggot."

The usher leaned forward and whispered in her ear. "First you gotta ball the Banger."

" 'S' all right. Him first. Gotta ball that Maggot."

By now, the other girls had realized that Vickie was Big Bang's chosen girl of the day and they crowded toward her, wondering if she were some famous groupie that they had not recognized. But her face was unfamiliar to them and after a few seconds' inspection, they decided that she was not their equal, that Big Bang Benton's taste was all in his ass, and they turned away. The usher took Vickie by the hand and headed toward a door in the corner of the room. At the door, he turned and called to the girls who were motionless, in that brief frozen moment before the stampede to the exits started, "Hang around, girls. I'll be back in a few minutes to tell you some inside stories about Big Bang and your other favorite stars." He smiled, cracking open a white-headed pimple on the side of his mouth, but the girls ignored that and squealed. Even an usher at an acid rock station was a celebrity.

The usher pushed Vickie through the door and began walking her down a long, rug-deadened hall, festooned with the station's initials. W-A-I-L. "Wail with Big Bang." "It's Big Banging Time at WAIL." In a series of framed advertisements behind glass on the walls idiotic slogans reduced Marconi's act of genius to its lowest common denominator. The advertisements were obvious allusions to sex, all happily seized upon by youngsters who wanted to embarrass their parents, without the concomitant danger of being responsible for the slogans themselves.

Vickie Stoner allowed herself to be propelled along the hallway, oblivious to the carpet, the signs and even the touch of the usher who was finding it difficult to resist a cheap feel, but did because of the possibility of reprisal from Big Bang.

"This is it, honey," the usher said, pausing in front of a wooden door with a gold star on it. "The Banger's inside."

"Gotta ball that Maggot," Vickie Stoner said.

She opened the door and walked inside. The dressing room was actually a small studio apartment, complete with refrigerator, stove, dining nook and bed. Big Bang Benton was in the bed, a sheet pulled up to his chin, staring at Vickie over his almost-black glasses.

"Lock the door, sweetie," he said.

Vickie Stoner turned and fumbled with the

lock button but did not know, or care, whether or not it locked.

"You're a loyal fan of the Old Banger, eh?" Benton asked.

"Do you know Maggot?" she asked.

"Maggot? One of my dearest and nearest friends. A great talent. Truly a star in the firmament of the music world. Why, just the other day, he said to me, he said . . ."

"Where is he?" Vickie interrupted.

"He's in town," Benton said. "But why worry about him. We're talking about you and me, the Old Banger."

"Gotta ball that Maggot," Vickie said.

"The way to his bed is through mine," said Benton.

Vickie nodded and began removing her clothes. In almost no time, she was stripped and crawling under the cover where she flopped down on top of Benton's porcine bloated stomach.

After it was all over, Big Bang decided it would be helpful to the girl to get to know her a little better. Perhaps show a little interest in her and let her know the big stars were just folks after all. So he talked to her about his hopes and his needs, his frustrations and his sense of accomplishment at bringing a little happiness into the lives of young America through good clean entertainment.

Before he could discover that Vickie was snoring, the telephone next to the bed rang.

He hesitated before reaching out to the telephone. But he was relieved to find out it was not his bookmaker, but the station's publicity department. He was supposed to meet Maggot later today at Maggot's hotel suite to present him with a gold record for the million-sales of

117

Maggot's latest and greatest hit, "Mugga-Mugga Blink Blank."

"Maggot say yes?" Big Bang asked.

"It's all set with him," the publicity man said.

"Gotta ball that Maggot," Vickie mumbled in her sleep, after hearing the magic name.

"All right," Benton said. "When and where?" He repeated the answer. "Hotel Carlton. Five-thirty. Got it."

He hung up the phone and was reaching for Vickie when the phone rang again.

There was no doubt about who was calling this time. Big Bang let out a heavy sigh, picked up the phone and sat up straight in bed to listen, lest his disrespectful slouching somehow show over the telephone.

"Yeah, Frankie, yeah. I understand." He tried a chuckle on for size, to lighten the tension. He felt Vickie Stoner stir and reached out a hand for her, but she eluded it, got out of bed, and began to dress. He waved to her not to go as he listened to Frankie. He winked at Vickie. "Frankie, you call at the damnedest times. I'm in the rack now with this sweet little red-headed groupie named Vickie and ... I don't know. Wait a minute, I'll ask. Hey, Vickie. What's your last name?"

"Stoner."

"I know you're stoned. What's your last name?"

"Gotta ball that Maggot," Vickie said and opened the door.

As the door closed behind her, Benton said, "I don't know. All she said was she was stoned." Pause. "I don't know. Maybe she said Stoner."

Then Big Bang listened, listened to what he had just had in his dressing room, listened to what she was worth, listened intently to how

118

some information on Vickie Stoner could not only wipe out his gambling debts but set him up for life, listened intently enough so that when he hung up, he raced naked out into the hall, looking both ways, but there was no sign of Vickie. Only a troop of visiting Girl Scouts from Kearny, New Jersey, all of whom seemed delighted at seeing Big Bang naked, but whose scout leader thought the display was obscene and marched off to complain to the station management.

Vickie was out on the street by that time. Something in her mind told her that Maggot was at the Hotel Carlton but she didn't know how she knew. Must have been an extra-good pill. The secret of all knowledge. Better living through chemistry.

Wobbly but decisive, she headed downtown, where she knew the Carlton was located.

Back at the studio, Big Bang reentered his dressing room and picked up the telephone. He gave the switchboard operator a number to dial and when it rang and was answered, he said: "This is the Banger. Let me talk to Maggot."

CHAPTER TWELVE

Calvin Cadwallader put the telephone down with a feeling of annoyance pervading his being, yeah, his inner being, right down to his innermost soul. That made him feel delighted. He promised himself that he would describe in great, glowing detail to his shrink the anger and annoyance he had felt, the curious theory being that after being annoyed, if one talked it out, the annoyance could be found not really to have existed.

But for now, there was annoyance. "If you see a red-haired groupie named Vickie Stoner, pick her up. It's important."

Things like that might be important to Big Bang Benton but Calvin Cadwallader knew better.

He touched his fingers to the sleeves of his brocade dressing gown, then ran his fingers lovingly through his freshly-curled blond hair, wiped them again on his sleeves and returned to the dining room of his eight room suite. The *Wall Street Journal* was open to the stock prices and Calvin Cadwallader, before he was interrupted, had been checking to see how he was doing.

He was doing very well indeed. That was one aspect in favor of being Maggot. But on the other hand, there were the headaches and the pressures and the feeling of lost identity. That was also because of being Maggot.

The psychiatrist had told him this was normal with someone who was leading two lives, and Calvin Cadwallader believed him because he was the only person in the whole world who loved Calvin Cadwallader for himself, and not just because seven nights a week and some days, Calvin Cadwallader donned terrible clothes and hideous makeup and festooned himself like a butcher shop to appear in public as Maggot, the leader of the Dead Meat Lice.

Maggot put on his white cotton gloves and then began again to run his finger down the columns of stock closing prices. Every so often, he would jot a number down on a light green ledger pad next to him, and then go into a flurry of high-speed calculations, the subject which he had been trained to excel in when he had gone to Rensselaer Polytechnic Institute. That was also where he had first picked up a guitar and forced himself to learn to play it, hoping it would help him overcome the crushing shyness which had been his ever since he had first realized that his globe-trotting parents hated him and wished him dead.

Maggot and the Dead Meat Lice started as a joke, a parody, a one-song routine in an RPI variety show. But someone in the audience knew someone who knew someone else and before you could say "shattered eardrum," Maggot and the Dead Meat Lice had signed a recording contract.

Fame, fortune and schizophrenia followed. Now Calvin Cadwallader considered both Calvin Cadwallader and Maggot as two separate and distinct persons. He vastly preferred Calvin Cadwallader. Still at times, Maggot was nice to have around because his music had made him very wealthy and he didn't care what Calvin Cadwallader did with the money.

Cadwallader had invested it wisely and well, specializing in oil and mineral stocks, but specifically excluding the string of companies owned wholly or in part by his father. He hoped they all went under, and even though it would have cost him hundreds of thousands, he wrote frequent letters to Congress, urging the elimination of the oil-depletion allowance on which his father's fortune had been built.

Morning computations done, Maggot rose from the table and went to a small bar-type refrigerator in a corner of the room. He extracted six bottles of pills, opened them, and began to count them out on a clean saucer he took from a closet.

Six vitamin Es, eight Cs, two multi-vitamins, four capsules of B-12, an assortment of tablets of wheat germ and rose hips, and high protein pills.

He capped the bottles tightly and replaced them in the refrigerator. Then he peeled off his gloves, so he wouldn't get lint on any of the tablets and began to pop them down, one after another, without water, the ultimate mark of skill for a pill popper.

He was five-feet-eleven, weighed 155, and he credited his pills with giving him a resting pulse rate of fifty-eight. He neither smoked nor drank; he had never used a drug; and he went to the Episcopal Church every Sunday, a feat made simpler by the fact that without his Maggot makeup and fright wig, and without lamb chops hanging from his chest, no one was likely to recognize this tall thin WASP as the singer that *Time* magazine had labeled "a cesspool of decadence."

Maggot walked toward the front of the suite, where the three Dead Meat Lice shared rooms and were probably playing cards, when the door bell rang once, timidly.

He looked around for a servant, saw none, and because he could not stand ringing doorbells or telephones, he picked up his white gloves, put them back on and opened the door.

A lissome, red-haired girl stood there. She looked at him dreamily and spoke softly.

"You're Maggot, aren't you?"

"Yes, but don't touch," said Cadwallader, who believed in the truth above all.

"I don't want to touch," said Vickie Stoner. "Let's ball," she said, and fell, slumping onto the floor. Cadwallader who barely had a chance to recoil and get out of her way lest her falling body

122

touch him, began to shout for the Lice to come and take care of her.

"Help. Strange woman. Help. Come quick." Maggot yelled the same words again, then turned and ran to the refrigerator to get calcium tablets, which he had been assured would be good for his nerves.

CHAPTER THIRTEEN

The land rover had been driven through the night, all the gas in the spare ten-gallon drum in the back had been used, and now when the vehicle crested a hill and the morning sun knifed into the eyes of the driver, he realized how tired he was.

Gunner Nilsson pulled off to the side of the narrow, rock-strewn dirt road. He hopped from the open rover and went to a nearby tree, where, using a handkerchief, he wiped morning dew from its low hanging leaves, and carefully washed his face and eyes. The cool feeling lasted only a few seconds before the handkerchief turned damp and hot and sweaty, but Nilsson redoused it again and washed his face again and then felt better.

It had taken a while for Lhasa to interest him in the project, but now Gunner Nilsson was fully committed to carrying out the million-dollar contract on the girl. A million dollars. It could build him a real hospital. It could buy him real medical supplies and surgical equipment, instead of the leftovers he now used. The million dollars could put meaning into his life and he was at the age when meaning was all that was left to his life.

He and Lhasa were the last of the Nilssons. There would be no more. No one to carry on the family name, or its sour tradition, but what better way for it to end than in a final act of assassination that would be a tribute to life, to humanity, to healing?

The end justified the means, at least in this case, just as the end had justified the means twelve years before, when he had operated on Lhasa for appendicitis and while the younger brother was out, had performed on him a vasectomy that would guarantee the extinction of the Nilsson killers.

As eldest, Gunner had been the keeper of the tradition, and he had determined that the tradition was not worth keeping. Except for this one contract. For all the good it could do.

Gunner Nilsson clambered back into the rover, no longer afraid of falling asleep at the wheel, and drove the steep three miles down the mountainside to the small waterfront village which had most of the necessities of life, including a telephone in the home of a British field officer.

Lhasa was to have telephoned a message to the field officer which should have arrived by now. It made a difference—being a millionaire medical missionary, or a penniless overeducated crank trying to bring healing to natives who were not ready for healing that did not involve the mask and the dance and the song.

Field Lieutenant Pepperidge Barnes was at home when Dr. Gunner Nilsson arrived; he was openly delighted to see the old man. He often worried about the kindly, harmless gentleman alone up there in the hills with those insane savages, and he had been meaning to drive up to see him.

No, there had been no message for Doctor Nilsson. Was it anything important? Oh, just a message from his brother on vacation? Well, of course, feel free to use the telephone. Lt. Barnes was going to walk to his office to see what mischief the retarded inhabitants of this retarded land had committed on Her Majesty during the night. Perhaps when Dr. Nilsson had completed his call and had rested, he would stop at Lt. Barnes' office and the two could play a game of chess?

After Barnes left, Gunner Nilsson sat for a long time, looking at the telephone, half-expecting it to ring. He did not consider it possible that Lhasa had failed. After all, he was a Nilsson with Nilsson instincts and Gunner had told him how to do it, and Nilssons did not fail. Still, he should have called by now.

Gunner waited, but after an hour elapsed he began the laborious process of placing a call to the number Lhasa had told him about in Switzerland.

He sat for another hour with the telephone in his hand, staring at his hand, taking satisfaction in the knowledge that it was old and tanned and had of its own volition put down the weapons which for six hundred years had been the legacy of the Nilsson family, father to son, generation to generation, century to century.

No more killing. Just this one by Lhasa and then no more.

He felt the telephone vibrate in his hand and he raised it to his ear.

"We have your number in Switzerland," the female voice said.

"Thank you," he said.

"Go ahead," she said.

"Hello," a man's voice said.

"I am calling in regard to certain moneys due to a Mr. Nilsson for performance of a certain service," Gunner said.

There was a pause, then the voice said, "Who is this?"

"My name is Dr. Gunner Nilsson. I am Lhasa Nilsson's brother."

"Oh, I see. Dr. Nilsson, I am sorry to have to tell you this. There will be no payment made on that contract."

Gunner Nilsson's hand tightened around the telephone. "Why?"

"The contract has not been concluded."

"I see," Nilsson said slowly. "Have you heard from Lhasa?"

"Again, I am sorry, Doctor. I have not heard *from* him. However I have heard of him. I'm afraid your brother has met with an untimely end."

Nilsson blinked hard. He caught himself doing it, and reacted by opening his eyes wide.

"I see," he said again. "Do you have any details on the matter?"

"Yes. But I am not able to discuss them on the telephone."

"Of course, I understand," said. He cleared his throat. "I will speak with you again in a few days. But now there is something you must do." He cleared his throat again.

"What is that?"

"Close the contract. I will carry it out myself. Without interference."

"Are you sure you wish to do that?"

"Close the contract," Nilsson said and hung up the phone without saying good-bye. His old and tanned hand rested on the telephone cradle. He picked up the receiver again. It fit smoothly in

126

the palm of his hand and was cool to the touch, just, he realized, like the butt of a revolver.

He sat there, sensing the warmth of the imaginary revolver in his hand, thinking of all the children Lhasa might have had who could have extracted payment from a world which had killed their father. But Lhasa had never had those children. Gunner had seen to that.

So what was left?

Gunner squeezed the telephone receiver, lifted it slowly and held it at arm's length, aiming the earpiece at a spot against the far wall. With his index finger he squeezed. For a moment, he felt the need to blink, but he suppressed it. How quickly the old habits returned. He cleared his throat as his finger pressed hard on the middle of the receiver. He smiled at the sound.

Lhasa would need no children to avenge him.

CHAPTER FOURTEEN

"That's right," said Remo. "We lost the girl."

He heard Smith choke on the other end of the phone.

"Nothing curable, I hope," Remo said.

"Don't worry about it," Smith said. "Have you any leads on the girl?"

"Maybe," Remo said. "There is some kind of a thing called Maggot which apparently is a singer. She's been looking for him. I think I might be able to find her there."

"It's imperative to keep her alive."

"Right," Remo said.

"And there are new complications."

"As opposed to the old complications?"

"The Lhasa Nilsson you ran into?"

"Yeah."

"He makes this international. An international contract."

"Doesn't matter," Remo said.

"Maybe it does," Smith said. "The Nilsson family is something special."

"In what way?"

"They have been in this business for six hundred years."

" 'This business' is killing?"

"Their reputation says they have never failed," Smith said.

"I have one stiff in the closet who's spoiled their record," Remo said.

"That's what worries me," Smith said. "I just can't believe it's going to stop there."

"And I told you it doesn't matter. One country, a hundred countries. One Nilsson, a hundred Nilssons. All the same. If we find the girl, she's safe."

"Are you really so arrogant?" Smith asked.

"Look," Remo said testily. "You worry about all the Nilssons. Worry about them all you want. Do you really believe there is any comparison between them and the House of Sinanju?"

"They are highly regarded."

"Come look in my closet. See what that does for your high regard."

"I am only suggesting that you be realistic and cautious. You are up against very good people and you sound like Chiun. The next thing I know you'll be telling me some nonsense about the majesty and worth and wonder of the House of Sinanju."

"You know," Remo said, "You don't deserve what you get. You deserve some heavy-handed button man who needs two assistants to read the name of the victim."

"Just don't be like Chiun."

"I won't. But don't expect the mountain to tremble at the breeze."

He hung up, feeling tense, disgusted by Smith's lack of confidence. He looked up to see Chiun staring at him from across the room, a small smile on his face.

"What are you smirking about?" Remo demanded.

"Do you know that there are times when I actually think you may yet amount to something?" Chiun asked.

"Don't get carried away," Remo said. "Come on, we're going to visit someone."

"May I ask who?"

"I hoped you would," Remo said. "We're going to see Maggot and the Dead Meat Lice."

"Only in America could I be so fortunate," Chiun said.

Vickie Stoner stuck out her tongue and took a long lick of the shiny red, translucent lollipop. It was being held in the right hand of Dead Meat Louse Number One, who sat on the edge of Vickie's bed.

"Just like being a baby again, man," she said.

"Even better," he said. "These ain't just any lollipops."

"No?"

"No. I buy them special." He leaned forward and whispered, "From the House of the Heavenly Hash."

"That's bitchen, man. Bitchen."

"Sweets for the sweet."

"Great, Number One. You just make that up?"

"Nahh. I read it once in a lyric."

"Cool," she said. "Why not climb in here with me?"

"Thought you'd never ask."

Louse Number One was wearing only a thigh-length dashiki which he peeled off quickly, before he slipped under the sheet with Vickie. He still held the lollipop in his right hand.

"You know, I'm gonna ball that Maggot," she said in his ear.

"Forget it, Vickie. Maggot won't ball. Germs or something."

"He'll ball. I just gotta figure out how."

"Hey, remember me? I'm the guy that put you back together again when you wandered in here with your head strung out behind you. I'm the one who chased that fat-ass disc jockey away by telling him you'd split. Remember me?"

"I never forget a favor, Number One, but I gotta ball that Maggot. Hey, what time is it?"

He handed her the lollipop as he looked at his watch. "Six o'clock," he said.

"No, not that time. Day of the week time?"

"Oh, it's like Wednesday or something."

"Well, you just stay here and wait for me a minute," she said, and put the lollipop on the black curly hair on his chest. "I gotta make a call first."

"I am pleased by what you told Dr. Smith," Chiun said.

"I can't understand him getting upset about somebody nobody ever heard of."

"You should not disregard his anxieties. It is difficult sometimes to deal with a new house. They have no traditions and therefore are not bound by custom."

"Well, I'm not going to worry about them. What I'm worried about is finding the girl. It's strange, you know. The people who are trying to kill her never seem to have any problem locating her."

"Maybe she is wired for sound," Chiun said. "I understand that is what your country does with important people."

"How can we protect her when we don't know where she is?"

"It happened once to another Master of Sinanju, but it all worked out well," Chiun said.

"How?" Remo said suspiciously.

"The Master was hired to protect someone. He did not know the whereabouts of that someone but the killer did."

"So, what happened?"

Chiun shrugged. "What you would expect. The killer killed that person."

"Then how can you say it worked out well?"

"It did. It was the fault of the emperor who hired the Master. No one blamed the House of Sinanju and the Master was paid anyway. So you can put your mind at rest. No one will blame us if something happens to the girl. And we will be paid."

Remo shook his head in wonder.

"Before we leave," Chiun said, "we must bury Lhasa Nilsson in a correct way. He is a member of a House."

"So?"

Chiun exploded in a babble of Korean. "So?" he said in English. "So he is a member of a House, a member of our profession. He must be buried ritually. I understand people from that part of the

131

world have a certain way of disposing of their warriors."

Remo thought back, remembered the movie *Beau Geste* and said, "Funeral by fire."

"Correct," Chiun said. "Please take care of it."

"How?" Remo said. "Call our friendly neighborhood funeral parlor?"

"I'm sure that to one who would understand the Secrets of Sinanju, such a thing would not be difficult. Please take care of it," Chiun said.

He walked away as Remo behind him mumbled, "Please take care of it, please take care of it," under his breath.

He watched Chiun walk into the bedroom where his steamer trunks were stored, then went to the closet and dragged out the green plastic trash bag containing Lhasa Nilsson.

He hoisted it up onto his shoulder and carried it out into the hall, mumbling irritably under his breath all the while. It was Gary Cooper in *Beau Geste*. But who was the brother who had the Viking funeral? Well, never mind. It was funeral by fire? But the suspicion nudged at him that there was something else.

What was it?

Remo looked both ways down the hall, then turned right. Halfway down the hall, he found what he was looking for, a large incinerator chute used by hotel workers for dumping waste.

What was that? What was it Gary Cooper had done? It was more than just funeral by fire.

Remo yanked the chute door open with his left hand and with a flick of his right shoulder twitched the bag onto the door. He was ready to push it down the chute, when a ferocious yipping sound pierced his ears and he felt needle pricks at his right ankle. Remo looked down. A Pomeranian dog with a jeweled collar was snapping at him. That's it, he thought. A dog. A dog has to go with the corpse in a Viking funeral.

From down around the corner, he heard a stentorian female voice whooping, "Bubbles. Where are you, Bubbles? Come to Momma."

But meanwhile Bubbles was doing a number on Remo's right ankle.

Remo flicked the trash bag containing Lhasa Nilsson into the chute. He heard it hiss as it slid through the metal cylinder, then whoosh as it fell free to finally thump as it hit in the basement.

The whooping crane who was looking for Bubbles was getting closer. Remo could tell because her voice had changed from a roar to a bellow.

He reached down and grabbed the fluffy ball of fur by the jeweled collar and extended his hand toward the trash chute.

"Oh, there you are," came the roar. Remo looked around to see a magnificently overupholstered woman in a black dress come thumping toward him.

She yanked Bubbles from his hand and turned and walked away, without thanks, murmuring endearments to the dog.

Oh well, Remo thought. The idea is what counts anyway. Lhasa didn't really need a dog to go with him.

Back in the room, he encountered Chiun coming out of the bedroom, having changed his robe from ceremonial blue to ceremonial green.

"All done," Remo said. "The Viking funeral is over."

Chiun raised an eyebrow. "Will his ancestors be pleased?"

"Yup," Remo said, doing his top impersonation of Gary Cooper.

"Good," Chiun said with a smile. "One must remember the traditions. Ashes to ashes. Dust to dust."

"And garbage to garbage," Remo mumbled, then said loudly, "He's on his way to Valhalla."

"Valhalla?"

"Yes, it's a hamburger stand in White Plains. Let's go, we've got to find Vickie Stoner."

"Must we go near this Maggot to do it?" Chiun asked.

"Of course. It's about time you saw the wholesome rich side of American life. We're going to broaden your horizons."

CHAPTER FIFTEEN

Maggot popped pills. A yellow C. An amber E. A pink B12.

"She's got to go," he said. He was wearing a white cotton bathrobe and his white gloves. A surgical mask hung loosely around his neck, its use unnecessary so long as Louse Number One, Number Two and Number Three kept a respectful distance from him, which they now did by sitting on the other side of the dining room table.

"But Maggot, she's all right," said Louse Number One.

"One groupie's the same as another groupie," Maggot said. "Why is she different, except that she spends all her time on the telephone?"

"In the first place, she's smart. In the second

place, she doesn't really get in our way. In the third place, if we believe that fat-faced wax spinner, somebody's trying to kill her."

"Well, let them," Maggot said. "I don't want to be killed by accident. Look, we've got two out-of-town concerts and then the big festival in Darlington. We just don't need the headache."

"I say we vote on it," said Dead Meat Louse Number One, who had seen Louse Two and Louse Three sneaking from Vickie's room on separate occasions.

"Fine," Maggot said. "Usual rules. I vote she goes."

"And I vote she stays," said Louse One. He looked to Two and Three. They shuffled uneasily in their chairs under his glance and Maggot's piercing stare. Maggot picked up a carrot strip and stuck it in his mouth. "Vote," he commanded.

"She stays," said Two. "Ditto," said Three.

"Another tie, Maggot," said Louse One. "Us against you. She stays."

Maggot bit another piece of carrot angrily. "All right," he said. "She stays for now. But keep her out of my sight. And get her ready because we've got to leave now for Pittsburgh."

"She's already packed," said One.

Abdul Hareem Barenga was being kept alive by tubes. They were in his nose, in his arms, all over his body, the staff resident at Flower Lawn Hospital explained to the consulting surgeon who had just arrived from Africa.

"Serious internal injuries, Dr. Nilsson," he said. "All we can do is try to keep him alive one way or another. Medication cuts the pain, but he's got no chance. He wouldn't live five minutes without the life-support gadgets here." He spoke while

135

standing at the side of Barenga's bed, paying no more attention to the injured man than he did to his wife's nightly report on his son's transgressions in kindergarten.

"I understand," Dr. Gunner Nilsson said. "Nevertheless, I'd appreciate the opportunity to examine him privately if I may."

"Certainly, Doctor," the staff physician said. "If you need anything, just ring the buzzer over the bed. The nurse will help you."

"Thank you," Nilsson said. He took off the jacket of his blue suit and slowly rolled up his shirtsleeves, wasting time while the other doctor replaced the patient's chart, made a perfunctory check of the life-support systems, and then finally left the room.

Nilsson followed him to the door, locked the door behind him, then returned to Barenga's bed and pulled the folding screen to shield the patient from view through the glass-windowed door.

Barenga slept heavily, deeply sedated. Nilsson opened his doctor's bag, pushed aside the .38 caliber revolver in it, and shuffled through it until he found the ampule he was looking for. He snapped the neck of the tiny glass vial, drained its contents into a hypodermic syringe, pulled a tube from Barenga's arm and roughly jammed the hypodermic into the light brown skin near the inside of Barenga's left elbow.

Within sixty seconds, Barenga started to stir as the adrenal gland fought the sedatives for control of his body and began to win.

He opened his eyes wide, in a kind of frenzy, as the unblocked pain accompanied consciousness. His eyes wandered the room madly, finally focusing, without recognition or comprehension, on Nilsson.

Nilsson leaned close to the bed. His voice was a harsh guttural whisper.

"What happened to Lhasa Nilsson?" he asked.

"Who he?"

"The tall man with the blond hair. He was looking for the girl."

"Old man. Old gook killed him. Awful."

"What's a gook?"

"Gook. Yellow man. Yellow."

"What was the yellow man's name?"

"Don't know."

"Was there anyone else?"

"Man who got me. White smart-ass. He a friend of the gook's."

"You have his name?"

"Remo."

"First or last?"

"Dunno. He just say Remo."

"Hmmm. Remo. And an old Oriental. The Oriental killed Lhasa?"

"Yes."

"With a gun?"

"With his foot, man. Lhasa had the gun."

"Where did it happen?"

"Room 1821. Waldorf."

"Was there a girl? A Vickie Stoner?"

"She was gone when we got there. The gook was protecting her."

Barenga's voice was coming slower and fainter now, his body weakening, while the fight raged internally between the pain-killing sedatives and the pain-intensifying adrenaline.

"Thank you," said Dr. Gunner Nilsson. He replaced the tube in Barenga's arm. From his bag, he fished two more ampules of adrenaline and refilled the syringe. That done, he jammed the needle hard into the leathery sole of Barenga's

137

left foot and shot the lethal overdose into his body.

"This'll make you sleep. Pleasant dreams."

Barenga twitched as the adrenaline overpowered the sedative. His eyes rolled wildly; his mouth tried to work; then his head dropped limply to the side.

Nilsson pulled back the curtain, went to the door, unlocked it, and left.

Room 1821, Waldorf. Well, it was not much but it would be enough. At least for the last of the Nilssons.

CHAPTER SIXTEEN

The prop plane landed at Pittsburgh Airport in a slight rain and the stewardess decided the man in the fourth aisle seat on the left was just rude. But that was the way it often was with foreigners.

He just sat there. He had ignored her when she asked if he wanted anything. He had ignored her when she brought around the tray of drinks. He had ignored her when she asked if she could bring him a magazine. He just sat there, clutching his black leather doctor's bag to his chest, looking intently through the window.

And when the plane landed, why he had just ignored the sign demanding that seat belts remain fastened, and he was moving toward the exit door before the plane rolled to a stop. She started to tell him to get back to his seat, but he looked at her in such a strange way she decided not to say anything. And then she was too busy keeping the other passengers in their seats to worry about it.

Gunner Nilsson was the first one off. He marched down the ramp of the plane like the god Thor himself, sure of where he was going, sure of what he was doing, sure in a way he had not been sure of his medical work for years.

For thirty-five years, he had in his mind been Doctor Nilsson. But now, he felt only like Gunner Nilsson, the last surviving member of the Nilsson family, and it brought him a new sense of responsibility. Titles come and titles go; stations in life change for better or worse; but tradition is tradition. It is rooted in the blood and while it might be hidden or even suppressed, a day comes and it emerges, stronger for having been rested. He had been a fool to think of building hospitals. As an act of penitence for what? For the fact that his family for six hundred years had been the best at what they did? That required no penitence from anyone. He was glad now that he knew it. It removed the murder of Lhasa's killers from the realm of revenge and made it professional, an act of ritual ceremony.

The rain was falling harder when he hailed a cab in front of the airport and told the driver to take him to the Mosque Theater in the aging heart of the aged city.

He pressed his face against the light-streaked window as the cab plowed along streets whose drainage systems obviously had been designed to handle the runoffs from a heavy spring dew. Pittsburgh was ugly, but then, he reflected, so were all American cities. It was not true, as radicals charged, that America had invented the slum, but it had raised it to the level of an art form.

The rain made it difficult to see well, but not

even the rapping of the car's pistons, the tapping of the valves, and the rumbling of the muffler could block out the noise when the taxi pulled up near the Mosque Theater.

The sidewalk and street were almost filled with teenage girls. Grim-faced policemen in dark blue uniforms, yellow rain slickers, and white riot helmets stood in front of the theater, doing ushers' work at taxpayers' expense, trying to keep the frenzied teenagers in the ticket purchase lines. The wet street glistened with the flashing overhead lights from the marquee: "TONIGHT. ONE NIGHT ONLY. MAGGOT AND THE DEAD MEAT LICE."

"Hey, it's somebody," one girl shouted as Nilsson's cab stopped in the street, just outside the main horde of teenagers.

Heads turned toward his cab.

"No, it's nobody," said another girl.

"Sure it is. He's got a cab, ain't he?"

"Anybody can have a cab."

Nilsson stepped out of the cab after paying the driver and tipping him twenty cents, which he felt was appropriate. He was met by the two girls. He pulled his collar up around his neck.

"You're right," the first girl said. "It's nobody." The girls turned away in disgust, the rain water streaming down their shiny, unpainted faces.

Before moving, Nilsson looked around quickly. The police had been too busy to notice him. Good. He turned his back on the theater and walked briskly away. He needed to think. He tucked the doctor's bag under his arm, to protect its precious contents with arm and shoulder, and began to walk along the pavement, his ripple-soled shoes squishing on those rare, level sections of the cracked, torn sidewalk. He must be careful not to step in puddles. Water on the bottom of his shoes could be wiped off; water inside shoes would squish and make it impossible for him to move silently if he had to.

He walked around the entire block, placing his feet carefully. Then, his mind made up, he crossed the street in front of the theater, walked around the groups of girls and toward the alley leading to the theater's side entrance.

"Hold it, Mac. Where you going?" a policeman asked.

"I'm a doctor," Nilsson said, intentionally thickening his foreign accent and holding his medical bag out for inspection. "Someone called me. Somebody's sick backstage."

The policeman looked at him suspiciously.

"Come, officer," Nilsson said. "Do I really look like a fan of Maggot and the Meatballs or whatever they are?"

Under his bushy moustache, the young policeman's mouth relaxed into a grin. "Guess not, Doc. Go ahead. Call if you need anything."

"Thank you, officer," Nilsson said.

He slipped into the backstage door and, as he expected, found a scene of total confusion and bedlam, except for one grizzled old watchman, who moved forward toward him.

"Can I help you, mister?" he said.

"I'm Doctor Johnson. I've been asked to stand by during the performance in case there are any injuries or illnesses."

"Let's hope not," the old man said.

Nilsson winked at him and leaned forward. He felt good. His socks were dry. "Don't worry," he said. "We haven't lost an idiot yet."

He leaned back and shared a generation gap with the watchman.

"Okay, doctor. If you want anything, holler."

"Thank you."

Stage hands were moving musical instruments into place behind the curtain, beyond which Nilsson could hear the throaty murmur of audience. But he saw no sign of anything that looked like Maggots or Lice. Then across the stage, in the opposite wing, he saw the red-headed girl. She was tall and pretty, but her face had an absolute blankness that he recognized as narcosis, from either overdose or continuous drug use.

As he peeled off his light trench coat, he looked carefully around. There was no sign of an American who looked like he might be Remo. No sign of the old Oriental. If they were the girl's bodyguards, they should have been there.

But there *was* someone watching the girl. She stood indolently near a panel from which stage lights were controlled. Two men standing in the center of the stage were watching her. One wore incredibly vulgar sports clothes, almost black eyeglasses, and a black hairpiece that looked no more natural upon his head than a clump of sod would have. He was speaking rapidly to a short squat man, wearing a snap-brim hat. The squat man listened, then turned and looked at the redhead. He turned back and nodded. Instinctively, probably unconsciously, his right hand moved up and touched his jacket near the left armpit. He was carrying a gun.

Nilsson knew that he had just seen a contract issued for the girl's death. And he, Nilsson, had directed that the open contract be closed. The presence of the squat man in the hat was an insult to the Nilsson family that could not be allowed.

Nilsson unlocked the snap on top of his doctor's bag and reached in with one hand, checking his revolver to make sure it was fully loaded and the safety was off. Satisfied with that, he placed the bag on a small table and shielding it from the view of anyone else in the backstage mob, he attached the silencer to it. Then he closed the bag again and turned back to the girl.

How easy it would be now, if she alone were his target. One bullet. The million-dollar contract would be completed. But it was more complicated than that. That was for the million, but for Gunner, there were the two men who had killed Lhasa. Remo and the old Oriental. He scanned the crowd again. Still no sign of them. So be it. If it was necessary to wait for them to show up, he would wait. And if it was necessary to keep the girl alive for that, then he would keep the girl alive.

And if the world needed a message that the Nilsson family did not take kindly to people interfering with contracts they had taken, well, then he would send the world that message.

Nilsson looked at the girl again. Her eyes still did not focus, and her body was slumped against the light panel. He walked casually across the stage. As he neared, he saw the girl's mouth was moving slightly, forming words to herself, "Gotta ball that Maggot. Gotta ball that Maggot."

As he stood by the girl, Nilsson saw the man with the hat nod and turn away from the stage. Nilsson's body tensed instinctively. The man came toward him, then brushed past Nilsson without seeing him and headed toward a small stairway that apparently led upstairs to box seats.

Nilsson waited a few seconds, then followed. At the top of the stairs, away from the protective muffling of the heavy fireproof curtain, the sound of the audience was deafening. The man had entered a small one-person box seat at the left-hand side of the stage, from which he would have an unobstructed view into the right wing backstage. The door to the box had a small glass panel in it and Nilsson could see the man seat himself, take off his hat, then lean forward on the brass rail, as if gauging the distance to the girl, whom Nilsson could see over the man's shoulder.

As Nilsson watched, he saw a flurry of excitement in the wings and then, wearing their satin suits from which hung steaks, chops, beef kidneys, and slices of liver, came what were obviously Maggot and the Dead Meat Lice. Their costumes were white and already the heat of the backstage lights was softening the cuts of meat and blood was beginning to run down the front of their costumes.

Despite his absorption with the man in the hat and Vickie Stoner, Nilsson had time to think to himself: *Incredible.*

Then there was a fanfare. The houselights dimmed, went up, dimmed again. The front curtains opened and out stepped the fat, wig-wearing man with the loud clothes and black eyeglasses. A cheer went up from the audience, now jammed in, over one thousand strong.

"Hi, kiddioes. It's me, the Big Banger here," he said into the microphone. "You all ready for a little musical banging?"

A cheer went up from the crowd, one thousand voices wailing and screeching. The man at the microphone laughed aloud. "Well, you've come to the right place," he shouted in an accent that

144

Nilsson pondered for a moment, then placed as American Southern, not knowing that New York City disc jockeys always sounded as if they had Southern accents. The worse the music, the stronger the accent.

"We're all gonna get a bang out of tonight's show," the man said, and then glanced up toward the box seat to his right. Nilsson saw the fat man's head nod slightly in the box seat just in front of him.

"We want Maggot," screamed a voice. "Where's the Lice?" came another.

"They rot-cheer," said Big Bang Benton. "They just carving up a few little pieces of meat among them. Lucky little pieces of meat," he leered.

The audience laughed, the girls openly, the boys more self-consciously. Big Bang Benton seemed pleased that he had stopped the catcalls and the demand for Maggot but he did not want to put up with it again. It was demeaning to a star of his caliber. He cleared his throat, raised his hands over his head officiously, and said:

"Kiddioes. It's that time. Let's hear it for ... the one ... the only ... the greatest ever since the world began ... Maggot and the Dead Meat Lice."

The theater erupted in sound. The lights dimmed even further and a giant spot hit the center of the stage curtain. As Nilsson had expected, the heavy man in the theater box leaned forward. Through the window, Nilsson saw the man's hand reach under his coat. Nilsson silently pulled open the door to the box and stepped inside. His shoes were noiseless as he moved down the carpeted steps toward the man. Big Bang Benton still stood framed in the spot of the light; the audience continued its frenzied cheering; the main

145

curtains remained closed. Faint lights illuminated the wings of the stage. To the right, Nilsson could see the red-haired girl, Vickie Stoner, in the same spot. Now Nilsson saw a glint of metal in the fat man's hand.

Nilsson reached into his doctor's bag and pulled out his revolver. He looked past the fat man and saw Big Bang look up toward the box. The heavy man began to raise his pistol. Nilsson stepped behind his chair. In one smooth motion, he dropped his medical bag and slapped his left arm around the fat man's neck. He yanked him backwards away from the rail so that if the gun dropped, it would land on the carpeted floor of the theater box. The man struggled until Nilsson put the barrel of the .38 revolver against the base of his neck and fired down into his torso. The silencer-equipped gun coughed faintly; the man shuddered and slumped in the crush of Nilsson's left arm. Dead. The man's gun dropped noiselessly at his own feet. Nilsson's bullet would remain in the man's body until police surgeons removed it but there had been no chance of it exiting and plunging into the audience.

The man was dead but Nilsson held his arm around the corpse's throat, feeling the power the murder had given him. How many years had it been. Twenty-five? Thirty? He had not raised a gun in anger. He had turned his back on a family history and what had it gotten him? A famous tradition with no one to carry it on, and a dead brother. As the man grew heavier in his arm, Gunner Nilsson decided something that he had always felt: he was the greatest assassin in the world. And he was doing now, in vengeance and in the full power of his genius and skill, what God had always meant him to do. The blood pounded

146

in his temples. Viking fury rose in his throat and he tasted the bite of anger because someone had dared to violate the closing of the contract.

And there at center stage in his purple jacket and his black eyeglasses was the imbecile who had ignored Gunner Nilsson's warning to the world: this job is mine, stay away. Big Bang or whatever his name was would need a lesson too. The curtains began to open. There on the stage wearing their charnel-house costumes were Maggot and the Lice. The audience went wild. The musicians just stood there. Girls jumped over seats and began clambering down the aisles. Reluctantly, Big Bang Benton began to move out of the center spot toward the side of the stage away from Vickie Stoner. Nilsson waited until the angle was perfect, then snapped off a shot from his .38 that ripped through the front of the Adam's apple of the disc jockey. Benton clutched his throat and staggered offstage. No one noticed him, and the bullet, after passing through his throat, buried itself quietly in a sand bag near the edge of the curtain.

Nilsson smiled. Big Bang would not use his voice again to offer someone a contract that the Nilsson family had closed.

Then Maggot hit a chord on his guitar, one heavy seventh chord that hung in the air of the theater and whose echo overwhelmed and quieted down the fans' noise. For a moment, the echo competed with the stillness of the audience and then over the silence was heard the plaintive haunting cry of the red-haired woman backstage:

"Gotta ball that Maggot."

The sound was buried as the music began. Nilsson raised his pistol again, looked down its barrel and planted the tip of it against Vickie

147

Stoner's closed right eyelid. He held it there momentarily, then smiled and lowered the pistol. The million dollars would come later. First, there must be Remo and the aged Oriental.

Gunner Nilsson walked out of the theater box, back into the hallway and headed for the front of the theater. They would not be here tonight, his two primary targets. He would watch and wait. He went down a long flight of stone stairs to the lobby of the movie house which had, as most movie houses, been elegant once, but was now just wilted.

The red carpet in the lobby was worn, and tan threads showed through it as Gunner Nilsson walked on dry shoes toward the front door. His mind was far away. He would have to call Switzerland again and tell them that anyone else who moved on the Vickie Stoner contract would end up like the man in the hat. He would have to find out where the Maggots, or whatever their names were, would be performing next, because he would follow them until the girl's bodyguards arrived. When he found them, he would extract his revenge. And then . . . but only then . . . the girl.

These things went through his mind as he walked toward the front doors of the theater and his mind was not fully on his surroundings and he did not notice the young white man coming through the door until he had bumped into him.

"Excuse me," Nilsson said.

The white man grunted.

Nor did Gunner Nilsson notice the old Oriental standing off to the side of the lobby, looking at still photographs of movies that were coming Tuesday and Wednesday back in 1953.

The Oriental noticed Gunner Nilsson however.

"Come on," Remo said to Chiun. "We've got to

keep an eye on Vickie if she's here." He noticed Chiun's eyes following the man who had just bumped Remo. "What are you staring at?" Remo asked.

"That man," Chiun said.

"What about him?"

"He bumped into you but did not blink," Chiun said.

"So what?" Remo said. "He didn't burp either."

"Yes, but he should have blinked."

"Maybe his blinker broke," Remo said, still looking out toward the street, where the man now stepped off into the rain. "What difference does it make?"

"To a fool, nothing makes a difference," Chiun said. "Just remember, that man did not blink."

"I'll carry the knowledge with me to the end of my days," Remo said. "Come on." He turned and walked rapidly toward the orchestra section of the theater. But Chiun lagged behind, still looking out toward the street, still thinking of the man who did not blink.

CHAPTER SEVENTEEN

"Good-bye, Remo."

Chiun and Remo had worked their way backstage. The policeman who guarded the stage door entrances in the private side aisles had been confused when the two men approached. The elderly Oriental spoke to the two officers and pulled their eyes to him and the white man who was with him vanished. Just vanished. And when they turned to look for the white man, he was nowhere to be seen. They looked back to the Oriental to question him and he was gone too.

On the other side of the door, Remo and Chiun looked around. Remo felt relieved when he saw Vickie Stoner leaning near a lighting control panel. Stoned but alive, he thought.

He started to move toward her, but Chiun held back, looking in wonderment at the busy backstage, people scurrying about, perhaps apparently in logistical support of the creatures who were out on the stage now, making subhuman electrical noises.

It was then that Chiun said, "Good-bye, Remo."

"Good-bye? What Good-bye?"

"The Master of Sinanju tarries no place where people sing *mugga, mugga, mugga, mugga*."

"Don't listen. Block your mind," Remo suggested.

"Easy for you, since your mind is always blocked. I am returning to our hotel."

"Chiun, dammit. Who knows what might happen here? I might need you."

"You will not. Whatever is going to happen has already happened."

"You know that for a fact?"

"I do."

"Who told you?"

"The man who did not blink." With that, Chiun turned and walked back through the door to the hallway, politely saying "excuse me" to the policemen who had almost convinced themselves that the two men they had seen before were merely apparitions, hysterical visions brought on them by the heavy music of Maggot and the Dead Meat Lice.

150

Remo watched the door swing shut behind Chiun; he shrugged and moved to Vickie Stoner's side.

"Great, aren't they?" he said.

"Bitchen, man. Bitchen." She looked around. "Hey, it's you. My one and only lover." Her face showed real happiness to see Remo.

"If you loved me so much, why'd you run away?"

"Hey, I had things to do and I know you wouldn't let me. Besides, somebody was laying a lot of shit on me about his television shows."

"From now on, you just stay with me. Don't get between Chiun and his television set and everything'll be all right."

"Whatever you say, Remo." She put an arm over his shoulder. "You missed all the fun."

"What fun?"

"Somebody shot the throat out of Big Bang Benton."

"That's fun?"

"Ever hear his radio show?" Vickie asked.

"No," Remo said.

"Him without a throat is fun."

"Anything happen to you?" said Remo, suddenly cautious and moving around in front of Vickie to shield her from the upstairs box seats which he noticed had a good view of backstage.

"No. I just been listening to my Maggot. Gotta ball that Maggot, you know."

"I know," Remo said. "I'm going to fix you up with him."

"You are?"

"Sure. But you've gotta come up with me now so I can get my plans underway."

"Well, man, I'd like to, but tomorrow's the Darlington Festival."

151

"What's that?"

"Just the biggest rock bash in the history of the whole world."

"You couldn't miss that, could you?"

"No way. No way."

"Okay, we'll go there tomorrow." Remo started to say more, but realized he could no longer even hear his own voice over the sudden roar of sound from the audience. Their voices had been a steady background rumble since he arrived, but now there was a new sustained, high-pitched unison scream. And then, prancing offstage came Maggot, wearing his white suit with the steaks and liver pinned to it, followed by the Three Lice wearing the same costumes, but with less gold braid.

Vickie took her arm from around Remo's shoulder and stepped forward toward Maggot.

"Hey, Maggot," she called. He looked toward her. "Come here. You've got to meet a man."

Maggot took one cautious step toward Vickie and Remo. "What happened to Big Bang?" he asked.

"Oh, don't worry about him," she said. "Nothing serious. This is Remo. I want you to meet him."

Maggot looked at Remo. He did not extend his hand. Neither did Remo. The three Lice moved up close behind Maggot.

"Pleasure, fellow," Maggot said.

"Likewise," Remo said. "By the way, that's a great outfit you're wearing. Who's your butcher?"

Maggot smiled fixedly, saying nothing. One Louse asked, "Vickie, is this guy a friend of yours?"

"My lover. My favorite lover," she said.

152

"Him? He's like ancient, man. And look at his hair."

"You make love with your hair?" Remo asked.

"Well . . . maybe you do."

Out front, the screaming was growing more intense. "Gotta go back," Maggot said. "Quiet down the animals."

"Throw them some raw meat," Remo said.

Maggot looked at Remo shrewdly for a split second, then led the three Dead Meat Lice back on stage. The screaming doubled and redoubled. Maggot bowed. The three Lice bowed. The audience screamed louder.

Maggot waved his hands for silence. The wave produced chaos, and a surge of bodies toward the thin blue line of policemen who ringed the front of the stage.

Maggot waved again. Another surge. From his chest, he ripped a two-pound porterhouse steak and held it high over his head. In the hot lights, the blood and juice was shiny and slick against the meat. More screams. Like a Frisbee champion, he scaled it out into the audience. Frenzy. Chaos.

Then in an orgy of meat distribution, Maggot and the Lice tore the chops and steaks from their clothes and tossed them out over the audience's heads. As the meat splunked down toward the floor of the theater, little pockets of girls knotted and began fighting for the morsels. It looked like T-bone day at the Salvation Army kitchen. But there were more girls than there was meat.

Maggot and the Lice, after denuding their uniforms, started offstage. The meat had been swallowed up by two dozen lucky girls in the audience. The rest were infuriated. They charged the line of policemen. The policemen, held, bent,

153

broke, and the girls poured like a human flood onto the stage and then out into the wings.

First, Remo had stood there with Vickie. Then the Lice and Maggot had joined them. Maggot was beginning to thank Remo for his brilliant concept about giving away the meat when Remo was caught in a maelstrom, a whirlpool of hot, sweaty, perfumed, almost-clothed bodies that swirled backstage like a wall of water.

Over the shrieks came the baritone voices of policemen, trying to clear out the audience. Remo felt himself pressed against the lighting-control panel. He turned toward it, felt hopelessly confused, grabbed as many switches as he could and began pulling them all down. The fifth one worked and backstage was plunged into darkness.

Screams became shrieks. Remo pinched his eyes shut for a second with his hands, forcing the pupils to widen, then he opened his eyes. He could see as well as if there were a light on, and he moved through the crowd of blinded tenagers and policemen as if they were not there. He moved toward the door to the alleyway. Vickie had gone. Maggot and the Dead Meat Lice were gone. He moved outdoors into the drizzling rain. Pulling away from the curb was a tan Rolls Royce, a gang of girls racing after it on foot down the street.

Vickie had gotten away again.

CHAPTER EIGHTEEN

Two phone calls concerning Vickie Stoner were made that night from Pittsburgh.

In a rundown hotel, Dr. Gunner Nilsson managed to convince the desk clerk to get him Switzerland, even though he had to put up a fifty dollar cash deposit before the clerk would complete the call. Nilsson took the call in the lobby, to make sure the clerk did not open the key to listen in.

He said simply, "This is Nilsson. Someone else was after the girl tonight."

He listened, then said, "All right, they were not yours, but if any of yours show up, the same thing will happen to them."

He listened again and said "The Darlington Festival? Then that is where this will all end. But I caution you. No more bunglers getting in my way. You might let that be known."

Then, "Thank you." Nilsson hung up and went to his room. He had to clean and polish his revolver. Tomorrow would be his moment. He must be ready.

"Who cares what the papers say?" Remo said into the phone.

Patiently, Smith tried to explain again. The body of Lhasa Nilsson had been found and identified. The press had dredged up his background and was now speculating that he had been in this country on a murder contract when he had met his own death. But now, the word was out in the underworld that the Nilsson family was in the country to take revenge against the killers of Lhasa.

"So I care what the papers say," Smith said. "It means that you and Chiun must be extra careful. Vickie Stoner is now being hunted down by one of the world's great assassins and so, apparently, are you. Be careful. And it would probably improve Vickie Stoner's chances if you could keep her in your sight for more than a minute at a time."

"Yeah, right, right, right," Remo said disgustedly.

"Where are you going to pick up the girl?" Smith asked.

"She got away from us tonight in a riot. But we'll nail her at the Darlington music festival and get her away."

"Be careful."

"Is worrying written into your job description?" Remo asked, but Smith had already hung up and Remo slammed the phone onto the cradle.

"Dr. Smith worries?" Chiun asked.

"Yes. It seems the Nilsson house is after us because of what you did to Lhasa Nilsson."

"Of course, they are," Chiun said, shaking his head sadly. "But that is always the way with upstart houses. They take everything personally."

"But we don't?" Remo said.

"You do, but I don't. It is the difference between the keeper of a tradition, and something the cat dragged in."

Remo was now as annoyed at Chiun as he had been at Smith.

"Well, you better go easy, Chiun. I understand these Nilssons are good. And they're no upstart house. They've been at it for six hundred years."

"Still upstarts," Chiun said. "The House of

156

Sinanju existed when the Nilssons were still living in mud huts."

"Well, Smith says be careful."

"You should take his advice," Chiun said.

CHAPTER NINETEEN

Being old hands at the rock festival routine, Maggot and the Dead Meat Lice, along with Vickie Stoner and their chauffeur, drove through the night to get to Darlington, a small village in the New York Catskills, where the concert would be held the next day.

Rooms had already been reserved at the town's one-and-only motel under the name of Calvin Cadwallader, and there Maggot and company would dress tomorrow before being helicoptered to the concert scene to do their bit. They would also leave by chopper. This approach had come through experience, because they might literally be dismembered if they allowed their bodies to get into the clutches of their adoring—mostly young, mostly female, but all predatory—fans.

As the car rolled heavily away from Pittsburgh, Maggot sat in the back of the Rolls, Vickie next to him. From a compartment alongside the door, he took a pair of white gloves which he put on as carefully and ceremoniously as if he were a professional pallbearer. From the same compartment came the *Wall Street Journal*, an early edition which he had flown to him wherever he happened to be.

He opened the paper to the New York Stock

Exchange tables, after flipping on the airplane-type light in the right rear corner of the car. He began to run a glove-covered right index finger down the columns of type, which were printed bigger in the *Wall Street Journal* than in most other papers which carried stock prices.

Every so often, he would grunt. Vickie Stoner sat as close to him as his sense of hygiene would allow. Once she had gotten really close and he had simply pushed her back to her side of the seat as if she were a bag of groceries that had fallen on its side. The three Lice sat in a seat in front of them, chattering about music, girls, music, girls, and money.

Calvin Cadwallader grunted again. His finger rested on the name of a conglomerate. He opened the doorside compartment again and took out paper and a ledger pad and wrote down a figure.

"Sell," said Vickie Stoner, who was able to see the name and number Maggot had written.

"Why sell?" Maggot asked. "It just went up a point." For a moment, he forgot that he was talking to an idiotic, sex-strung groupie.

"That's right," Vickie said, "and it's selling at thirty-six times earnings. And there's a Japanese company that's making a breakthrough on this out-fit's main product and can produce it for half the cost. So sell, while you can still get out with a profit."

She turned away from Cadwallader and looked through the window at the darkened, dismal Pennsylvania countryside.

"Why didn't my business manager tell me that?" Cadwallader asked.

"Probably he doesn't want you to sell until he unloads his first. Would you blame him? Sell."

"How do you know so much about the

158

market?" Cadwallader asked. "That is, if you do know anything about the market."

"Right now, Maggot," Vickie said, enjoying seeing him wince at the name, "I am worth seventy-two million dollars on the hoof. No one who is worth that much money is allowed to be ignorant or stupid. When my father dies, I should be worth a quarter of a billion dollars. Somebody's got to mind the store."

Cadwallader was impressed. He began to rattle off the names of stocks. "Tell me the truth," he said. "Your honest opinion."

He named a soft drink company.

"Sell. The Russian contract is falling through."

A drug company.

"Buy. They've got an oral contraceptive for men."

A petroleum company.

"Sell. There's been a change in the return-of-capital ruling on their dividends. After September first, you'll go for your lungs in income taxes."

They discussed high finance all the way to Darlington. They ignored the Dead Meat Lice and talked all the way into the motel parking lot.

They were finally interrupted when the giant sedan rolled to a stop in front of the string of rooms they had rented. Maggot got out, followed by Vickie.

"Take the car over to that guest house on the other side of town," Maggot told the driver. "But don't forget. Be back here at exactly five o'clock tomorrow. Have everything packed and the motor running. That's when our helicopter will get back from the field."

"Yes, sir," the driver said. He took a string of bags out of the trunk, put them on the ground, and then drove quickly out of the lot, lest anyone see and recognize the car.

Maggot and the Lice already had their room keys. As they walked toward the string of rooms, Louse Number One fell in alongside Maggot.

"We all set for tomorrow?"

"Right," Maggot said.

"Need any rehearsal time tonight?"

"No," Maggot said. "I don't have time."

"You don't have time? What's so important?"

"Gotta ball that Vickie," Maggot said. He walked away from the stupefied Louse and followed Vickie into her room; he was already fishing inside his small personal-items kit for his jar of Vitamin E capsules.

Not being old hands at rock concerts, Remo and Chiun left the next morning for Darlington, before the sun rose, and found that everyone in the Western world had had the same idea. Twenty miles from Darlington, the traffic stopped.

Like an ant trying to find his way past a puddle, Remo turned from road to road, from highway to back street, from throughway to country road. All the same. All filled to overflowing. No one moved.

It was 10 A.M.

Chiun sat looking out the passenger's window which was open, allowing the air conditioning to rush out, unimpeded by the complication of cooling Remo at all. "The highway system in your nation is very interesting," Chiun said. "It works perfectly well until someone decides to use it. It must have taken much planning to build roads that are too big for light traffic and too small for heavy traffic."

Remo grunted. He wheeled the car around and

put it back onto the main highway. Still twenty miles to go to Darlington. Only three hours before the concert started.

Remo sat stalled in traffic. A black and white police car whizzed alongside him on the shoulder of the road, its overhead light whirring, its siren whooping occasionally.

Up ahead, Remo could see the first signs of disintegration of the crowd's discipline. People were getting out of their cars. Some were climbing on car roofs to play cards. Others were beginning to huddle together, rolling marijuana joints. Car doors opened as if a fire drill had been called. Remo groaned. The traffic would never move now.

"Perhaps if we walk," Chiun said. "It is a good day for strolling."

"Perhaps if you just leave things in my hands, we will get there," Remo said sharply.

"Perhaps," Chiun said. "And then again . . ." he added. But Remo did not hear the rest of the sentence. He was watching in his rearview mirror the approach of another police car. This one was an unmarked Chevrolet, a red light flashing inside the car on the dashboard. It gave Remo an idea. He said a few words to Chiun.

Both got out of their car and moved over onto the road shoulder. Remo waved his arms over his head at the onrushing detective's car, which finally screeched to a halt near Remo's toes.

The driver rolled down his window.

"What the hell are you doing, Mac?" he shouted. "Get out of the way. This is police business."

"Right," Remo said, approaching the driver. "Right you are." Chiun walked around to the passenger's side of the car.

Remo put his hands on the driver's door,

161

noting with dismay that the passenger's side door was locked. "But listen, man," Remo said, "like wow, this is important too."

"Well, what is it?" the detective said anxiously, moving his right hand across to the left side of his rumpled gray suit.

"It's important, I tell you," Remo said.

The policeman looked at him, his attention totally distracted from Chiun.

"So?" the cop said.

"Man, I want to make a citizen's arrest. You see all these people around here. Man, they are all smoking pot. Now, unless I miss my guess, that is against the laws of New York State and Nelson Rockefeller. I mean, man, like all these people, they ought to be good for seven to fifteen under your new law. I want to swear out a warrant for their arrest."

The policeman shook his head. "Can't do anything about it, fella. We've been told to lay off."

"Is that any way to build respect for the law?" Remo asked.

"Those are the rules," the detective said.

"In that case," Remo said, "have you got a match? I mean, the lighter's like busted in my car and my grass is just sitting there, getting old and cold and sad and old. If I don't get a match, I'm just gonna waste away."

"Waste, you son of a bitch," the policeman said. He jammed the car angrily into drive and sped off, his rear wheels kicking gravel and pebbles back at Remo and Chiun.

Remo watched him leave, then turned to Chiun.

"You get it?"

Chiun brought his hand from behind his back.

It held the red blinking light from the car's dashboard.

"How'd you open the door?" Remo said. "It was locked."

"Clean living," explained Chiun.

"Let's go," Remo said.

Back in the car, Remo wired the light to the two clips behind the cigarette lighter of his rented auto. The light began to rotate and flash.

Remo pulled off onto the shoulder, stepped on the gas and zoomed off toward Darlington. Acid rock freaks waved at him as he sped down the road. Some of them, already stoned, wandered out into the shoulder of the road and Remo was forced to swerve his way through them like an open field runner.

"Not so fast," Chiun said.

"Concentrate on the centrality of your being," Remo suggested.

"What does that mean?" Chiun asked.

"I don't know. It's what you always tell me."

"And good advice, too," Chiun said. "I shall concentrate on the centrality of my being." He lifted his legs up onto the front seat of the auto and folded them into his meditation position. He stared straight ahead out the window. Ten seconds later his eyes were closed.

Remo would have sworn Chiun was asleep, that is, until he almost sideswiped a car moving out onto the shoulder, and Chiun said:

"Careful, lest you kill us both and leave Mr. Nilsson with nothing to do." As he spoke, he opened his eyes and looked out the side window. An elderly man with gray hair, carrying a doctor's bag walked rapidly along the shoulder of the road. Chiun saw him, watched him for a moment and nodded to himself. He turned toward Remo but

163

Remo had not seen the man. Chiun started to speak, then changed his mind and closed his eyes again. Why tell Remo anything? Particularly about an upstart House.

Gunner Nilsson looked up at the car whizzing past him and felt a distaste for soft Americans. Walk where they could run; ride where they could walk. No matter. Only a few miles left and he had plenty of time. Today he would not fail.

Maggot had breakfast in bed, Vickie at his side.

"What do you really think about Christmas trees as a tax shelter?" he asked, munching on a soy-flour roll.

"Not bad, if you're prepared to wait five years for some return," she said. She reached toward her canvas bag and fished a hand inside it. She pulled out a vial of blue pills and her face lit up with pleasure.

"Why not eat?" Maggot said. "There's plenty for both of us."

"Sure, Maggot, sure. But I always have my morning tonic."

She took out one of the pills, but on its way to her mouth, it was intercepted by Maggot's hand.

"Eat, I said." He tossed the blue pill off toward a corner of the room, then picked up a roll and stuffed it into her mouth.

Vickie Stoner looked at Maggot with a new sense of appreciation. In bed, he wasn't much, nothing like that short-haired straight, Remo. But the thoughtfulness was nice.

"Come on," Maggot said. "Eat that roll and let's kick around those soybean futures."

164

CHAPTER TWENTY

The sun was high and the air was still and the heat lay over the twenty-five-acre concert site like an airproof iron blanket.

Remo and Chiun moved slowly through the grounds, looking for the bandstand.

"Where's the bandstand, pal?" Remo asked a young bearded man, who sat cross-legged on the ground, rocking back and forth.

"What bandstand, man?"

"The place where they're going to play."

"Yeahhhh, they going to play and I going to listen."

"Right. But where?"

"I going to listen right here. In my ears. My pretty pearl-drop ears that hear all the good and reject all the evil. In with the good and out with the bad." He giggled. "That's my secret formula for artificial respiration."

"And what's your secret formula for lunacy?" Remo asked in disgust. He turned away and continued walking with Chiun.

"Very enlightening," Chiun said. "They come to see and hear but they do not know who or where. It is very interesting, how clever you Americans are. And what is this smoke that covers these grounds?"

"It is just burning grass," Remo said maliciously.

"It does not smell like burning grass," Chiun

165

said. "Yet if it is, why is no one afraid? Do they not fear fires?"

"If you burn enough grass, you're not afraid of anything," Remo said.

"That answer makes no sense," Chiun said.

Remo looked pleased. "It's vague only to you."

A quarter of a million people had already jammed into the site and more were marching in every moment, making movement almost impossible. All pretense of ticket taking had stopped and now field and concert area was just open country. The promoters of the concert had made their money on advance sales, and with that in the bank, they did not care how many freebees ripped them off for admissions.

The old farm area was now a sea of dots, each dot a cluster of three or four or five people, some sitting on the ground, some lying on air mattresses, others in pitched tents. Normally, Remo would have looked to see which way the tents were facing, but these small groups were formless, pointed in no direction, having come not to see or hear but to be seen and to be heard. Each protected his own little piece of turf, and Remo and Chiun drew dirty looks, a few curses and much mild abuse as they moved through the little pockets of territoriality, looking for the stage.

Up ahead, Remo heard a motorcycle rev up, start up with a cough, then roar the engine into warmth.

"We're going right," he told Chiun.

"How do you know that?"

"Find the motorcycles and you find the stage," Remo said.

"It is part of the music?" Chiun asked.

"No, but the sounds are almost indistinguisha-

166

ble," Remo said. Resolutely he moved ahead, Chiun behind him, his head swiveling around, looking in wonder at the flow of humanity there.

"Look, Remo," he said. "That one is wearing the costume of your Uncle Samuel."

"Swell," said Remo, without looking.

"And there is Smokey the Bear."

"Great."

"Why is that one wearing a General Custer uniform? And there is a gorilla suit."

"Terrific."

"Why do you not pay attention? As the youth goes, so goes your country. Do you not want to see your people's next generation of rulers? Look! There is a boy dressed as Mickey Mouse and a girl dressed as Donald Duck."

"Good. What are they doing?" Remo asked, still moving forward.

"I would rather not say," Chiun replied. He speeded up his steps to come alongside Remo. "If this is what the next generation of rulers will look like in your country, I think you and I should begin looking for a new emperor," Chiun said.

"I agree," said Remo. "Just as soon as we get Vickie Stoner out of here in one piece."

"And settle with Mr. Nilsson," Chiun said.

"You think he'll be here?"

"I know he will be here."

"Well, keep your eyes open for him," Remo said smartly.

"Keep your eyes open for him," Chiun mocked. "No, I will keep my eyes closed."

The two had gotten past the last clustered clump of bodies now, and were standing alone on a fifteen-foot grassy strip that ran in a huge semicircle at one end of the property. At one side of the grassy band were the customers of the rock festival; fifteen feet away at the other side, a long string of motorcycle bums, wearing their leather jackets, standing almost elbow-to-elbow in front of their machines, trying to look tough. Behind them rose the stage, elevated 15 feet in the air. Sound towers rose on both sides and in the back, to pump the sound out over the entire area.

Remo and Chiun moved forward.

"Hey, you. You're in no man's land. Beat it."

The speaker was a black-suited motorcycle rider who stood facing them. His voice brought three or four others to his side. They were wearing identical costumes. On their peaked gestapo hats, Remo could read the legend: "Dirty Devils."

"It's all right," Remo said. "We're friends of the owner."

"That don't mean nothing to me," the loud-mouth said.

"Well, that means it must mean something," Remo said. "Don't you remember from school: negative double causes trouble? Sister Carmelita taught me that. Didn't you learn that in school? That is, if you went to school. Did they have school at the zoo?"

"All right, buddy. You and the old gent there, move on out."

"I'll give you a nickel if you let us pass," Remo said. "Just think. A nickel of your own. You can get your own bag of peanuts, and maybe your friends'll shell them for you."

Chiun put a hand on Remo's shoulder. "We may wait. There is no one here yet and there will be plenty of time."

Remo looked at Chiun, thoughtfully, then nodded. He turned back toward the four leather-clad cyclists. "Got you, fellows. See you later."

He turned and stepped back with Chiun out of

the no-man's-land ring of grass, into the tightly packed cluster of young people.

A little blonde girl jumped to her feet and embraced Chiun. "It's Bodhi-Dharma come to life," she said.

"No. I am only Chiun," Chiun said.

"You didn't come to take me to the Great Emptiness?" The girl seemed hurt.

"One can take no one to the Great Emptiness. Because to find it is to fill it and then it is emptiness no more."

"Well, if that's so, what sense does Zen make?" the girl asked. Around her feet sat three other girls, all mid-teens, their eyes all slightly vague, Remo noted. The ground around them was littered with what the unsophisticated eye might have perceived as tobacco ashes and cigarette butts.

"Another master was once asked that question," Chiun said. "He beat the questioner with a stick and then said, 'Now I have explained Zen.' It is, child, no more difficult than that."

"Bitchen, man, bitchen. Sit down with us and tell us some more. You too, man," she said to Remo.

Chiun looked at Remo, who shrugged. One place was as good as another and this one was close to the bandstand, which would be helpful when they had to make their move later. Chiun sank slowly into a lotus position on the ground. Remo dropped down next to him, drawing his knees up to his chin, watching the crowd, his concentration drawn away from Chiun and the four girls.

"You study Zen?" Chiun asked the blonde.

"We try. We all do, but we can't understand it," she protested.

169

"That is its point," Chiun said. "The harder one tries, the less one understands. It is when you stop trying to understand it that it all becomes clear."

Remo felt himself drawn back to the conversation by that lunacy. "That doesn't make any sense, Chiun," he said.

"Nothing makes sense to you except your stomach. Why do you not leave me and these children of peace and find yourself a hamburger stand where you may poison yourself?"

Remo sniffed, his feelings hurt, lifted his chin and turned his head away again without looking at the field.

Without looking at his watch, he knew it was five minutes to one. The concert was due to start soon.

As Remo watched the nearby crowd, Chiun talked, his voice hushed and muffled against the steady rumbling of voices from the quarter-million people gathered in the vast meadow. Occasionally, the buzzing, like a far-off train, would be broken by a shout . . . a scream . . . sometimes voices raised in song, singing almost in unison. Remo recognized the characteristic smell and noted for the first time that marijuana smoke drew mosquitoes. They were all over and one of the most persistent sounds throughout the field was hand slapping arm. Only Chiun seemed untroubled, even though the girls were smoking pot as he lectured. Remo felt more people around him. Their intimate group was growing larger. More and more persons had come to sit around the central cluster and listen to Chiun.

"Are you a priest?" one girl asked.

"No. Just a wise man." Remo snickered, and Chiun glared.

"What do you do?" he was asked.

"I raise money to feed the starving babies of my village," Chiun said, oozing humility and love, enjoying the moment.

"Tell them how you do it," growled Remo.

"Pay him no mind," Chiun told the group, which had now grown to a semisilent two dozen, squatting on the ground before him. "You have heard the Zen koan of the sound of one hand clapping. Next to you, you witness an even greater riddle: a mouth that works continually without connection to a working brain."

There were a few giggles. Everyone turned to look at Remo, who thought of answering but could not think of an appropriate retort.

Remo heard the first noises, that familiar rhythmic sound. A minute later it became audible throughout the field. Tension almost rose in waves as the sound of voices became louder. The excitement moved from a far corner of the farm property, across the field, ripping through the 250,000 people, tensing them all up, all of them talking at once. *They* were coming. They were coming. There it was. Their helicopter. It was Maggot. And the Lice. They were on their way. People stood and stretched their necks to try to see the chopper approaching. A few seconds later it swept into view.

A quarter of a million people saw it at the same time, and they vented their pleasure in a massive roar that made the ground Remo sat on tremble. But at Chiun's feet, the two dozen young people sat unmoving, listening only to Chiun as he spoke gently of love and honor in a world filled with hate and deceit.

Remo watched the helicopter. So also, for a few seconds, did Gunner Nilsson, who stood in front

171

of one of the guards at the far left side of the raised stage.

"I am the doctor hired by the owners," Nilsson said, lifting his bag for emphasis. "I must be near the stage."

"Man, I got no instructions about you," the Dirty Devil said. One other cyclist moved, as if to come over to lend support, but the first one waved him back. Who needed help handling a sixty-year-old man?

"Well, I have my instructions right here," said Dr. Gunner Nilsson.

The helicopter was now overhead. The guard glanced over his shoulder to watch the chopper start its descent in a large empty area between the stage and a stand of trees that marked the end of the farm property.

Nilsson opened his doctor's bag, reached his right hand in and gripped a hypodermic syringe. He waited until the guard's attention was on the chopper, and then slapped the syringe through the leather jacket into the young man's left bicep.

The needle bit flesh. Gunner Nilsson depressed the plunger. The guard turned, an angry look on his face, his hand reaching up to his arm, a curse on his mouth. His mouth opened to speak. It froze there momentarily, and then he fell, collapsing all at once.

The thump of his body on the ground drew the attention of the guard at his left.

"Quick," Nilsson said, "I'm a doctor. This man must be taken to the medical tent."

The guard looked at his fallen partner.

"Heat exhaustion, I think," Nilsson said. He waved his medical bag at the other guard. "Hurry. He needs treatment."

172

"All right," the man finally said. "Harry, give me a hand here," he said to the guard next to him.

Nilsson moved past the unconscious guard and toward the high, twice-twisting steps that led onto the left side of the empty stage.

The helicopter was on the ground, twenty feet behind the stage. Gunner Nilsson went up the steps and walked to the first landing, from which he could see over the heads of the motorcycle goons who ringed the front of the stage area. The crowd was on its feet now, standing, jumping, trying to get a peek at Maggot and his crew, but no one was willing to come forward across the no man's land separating the audience from the performance area.

Nilsson looked out into the crowd and saw it as a mass wave of humanity, impelled by idiocy and stupidity. How sad, how many people had to come together like this, just to prove to themselves that they existed.

As he looked at the wave of humanity, he saw a quiet, unmoving eddy of stillness. A group of twenty young people were sitting on the ground, many with their backs to the stage, at the center of them was an elderly Oriental in a saffron robe, his hands folded, his mouth working as he spoke. To the side of the Oriental, Nilsson could see an American, a youngish athletic-looking man who seemed to be counting the house.

Nilsson felt excitement raise gooseflesh behind his shoulder blades. His instincts told him who they were. The Oriental and the Remo who had killed Lhasa. They would be first. And then Vickie Stoner for the million and a half dollars. That was important now, because unless that

173

contract were completed there would be no meaning to Lhasa's death.

Nilsson rested his doctor's bag on a bannister made of a rough four-by-four and opened it. Inside the bag, his hands carefully checked his revolver.

Down below, in the eddy of serenity amidst the ocean of confusion, noise, and chaos that swept the field, Chiun sat and talked. And watched and saw.

"The secret of the world is to see," he said, "not just to look. One man looks at another and can see nothing. But another man can look and can see. He can see, for instance, that a man does not blink. It sounds like a nothing but it is a something. What if a man does not blink? He does not blink because he has been trained not to blink and it is good to know that a man has had that kind of training, because then you know what kind of man he is."

His high-pitched voice rambled on, Remo kept watching the crowd, looking for anyone who might be Nilsson. Random words and phrases moved into his consciousness. "The man who does not blink . . . dangerous . . . one should not just look but one should see."

Chiun was telling him something. What? He looked at Chiun, whose eyes met his. Chiun lifted his head toward the direction of the bandstand. Remo followed his eyes, and then saw the man on the steps, looking out toward Chiun. Remo had seen the man before when he had bumped into him in the Pittsburgh theater lobby.

Gunner Nilsson, here to kill Vickie Stoner. But why wasn't he turned toward the helicopter that had just set down lightly on the ground behind

174

the stage? Vickie would come from there. She would be defenseless.

Remo moved smoothly to his feet. "I go, Little Father. Do you join me?"

"I will stay here to entertain our friend."

"Be careful."

"Yes, Doctor Smith," Chiun said, a small smile on his mouth.

Remo moved sideways through the crowd which was now standing. He shortened his body, trying to melt into the mass of people. He started left, then moved right again, toward the no man's land on the other side of the stage from Nilsson. As he got closer to the fifteen-foot-wide grassy strip, Remo could see Maggot, the Dead Meat Lice, and Vickie Stoner standing on a platform under the stage. There was machinery there too. Probably some kind of elevator, Remo realized.

Remo stepped across the swatch of grass separating audience from stage. Most of the guards had their backs to the audience now, watching Maggot themselves, violating the first rule of the bodyguard trade.

The stage now blocked Nilsson from Remo's view. Remo moved behind one guard and placed his hand behind the man's neck. If anyone were watching, it looked like a friendly arm draped around a friend's friendly shoulder. The view of the audience did not include a look at Remo's fingers, which had moved into the thick neck muscles of the guard and quietly gripped a major artery carrying blood to the brain.

Three seconds and the guard went limp. Remo propped him against the tree he had been standing under and moved off toward the elevator platform under the stage.

On the steps on the far side of the stage, Gunner Nilsson took his pistol from his doctor's bag and dropped down onto the platform floor. Slats shielded him from the view of the audience, but he could see through the audience clearly. He poked the barrel of the revolver through one of the slats and zeroed the weapon in on Chiun, who sat placidly, continuing to talk, lecturing the young people around him.

Where was the white man? That Remo? Nilsson looked through the slats, left and right, but saw no sign of him. Well, no matter. He would not be far away. First the Oriental.

He aimed the point of the barrel at Chiun's forehead, just testing. But the forehead was not there. It was to the left. He moved the barrel of the gun again slightly to the left and fixed it on the forehead. But the forehead was again gone. It was below the line of his fire. He lowered the barrel. How could this be? The Oriental had not moved. Gunner was sure of that. And yet, he was never in the line of Gunner's fire.

That told him something, something out of the dim history of his family. What was it? A saying. He searched the corners of his mind but he could not find the answer. What was that saying?

Then he had no chance to think. The loudspeakers blared with a sound like God announcing the arrival of Judgment Day.

"Friends," a voice screeched. "People. Human beings all. We give you Maggot and the Dead Meat Lice." The last six words were delivered in a scream so amplified it could have brought a Latin American country to a halt.

Gunner held the revolver at his side and stood up. On the stage smoke was rising heavily, Gunner could see, from chemical pots hung under the stage surface. The smoke began to cover the

176

stage, heavy clouds of red, yellow, green, and violet, all merging smoothly in the hot still summer air. Gunner could hear machinery start. The lift below the stage was rising. He continued to watch the stage.

There was another sound. A giant vacuum began to suck away the smoke. It cleared almost instantly and there, standing on the stage, were Maggot and the three Lice. Behind them was Vickie Stoner. She would be last, however, Gunner thought to himself.

The girl backed away from the four-man group and suddenly, with a screech, Maggot and the Dead Meat Lice were into their first song. "Mugga, mugga, mugga, mugga," they wailed. The audience screamed, drowning out the amplification, making it impossible for anyone to hear the musical group the quarter of a million persons had traveled what came to millions of miles to hear.

Remo's ears pounded. He moved under the platform toward the steps on the left and hit them lightly on his way up.

Eight feet above Remo, Gunner Nilsson felt the boards shake. It was not the vibrations of the music, because he had already registered that sensation and filed it in his mind. It was a different kind of vibration; Gunner turned and looked down. Eight feet below him, at the bottom of the steps, was the American, that Remo.

All right. The American would be first.

Remo took a step up the stairs.

"Your brother blinked, you know," he said.

"Yes, but that was my brother," Nilsson said. He slowly raised the pistol on a line with Remo's chest.

177

No one saw; all eyes were on Maggot and the Lice.

Remo came up another step.

"He cleared his throat too, when he was ready to make his move."

"Many people do," Nilsson said, "but I do not."

"Funny," Remo said taking another step. "I kind of thought it was a family trait. You know, one of those weaknesses that are bred in and eventually wind up killing everybody."

"Anything that is bred in can be trained out," Nilsson said. "I do not have my brother's bad habits."

He smiled slightly as Remo came up another step. The American fool thought he was being so clever advancing slowly on Gunner Nilsson. Did he think for a moment he would have advanced if Gunner Nilsson had not chosen to let him?

There was a thing he wanted to know. He had to raise his voice to be heard over the roar of music.

"How did you kill him?" he called. "By his own gun?"

"Actually, no," Remo said. "I didn't kill him at all. Chiun did."

"The old Oriental?" That confirmed what the black had said, but Gunner still could not fully believe it.

"Yes," Remo said. "I think he took him out with a toe thrust to the throat, but I can't really be sure because I wasn't there." Another step.

"That is a lie. Lhasa was too big for the old man to handle alone."

"Wrong, Nilsson," Remo said. "That's the trouble with you squareheads. You never learn anything. I should think you'd have learned your

178

lesson by now. It's not the first time you've faced the old man."

Nilsson searched his brain. "Chiun?" The name meant nothing. "Never have we met him."

"But his ancestors," Remo said, taking another step. "At Islamabad. The Master of Sinanju."

Nilsson's face paled. "I have heard of such a one. It is now only a legend."

"He lives and breathes," Remo said. Another step.

"Not for long," said Nilsson, but his face turned white as he remembered the saying he had been searching his brain for. It had been handed down through generations of Nilssons.

"Where walks the Master from the East, let all other men give way."

Remo saw the blood drain from Nilsson's face. "You sure you don't blink or clear your throat? Or what's your weakness? From the looks of it, perhaps you just have a coronary."

Another step. He was too close now. Nilsson closed his finger about the trigger. It went off with a crash, loud, piercing, but still unheard against the rumble of the music. The white man dropped. He was dead. No, he was not. He was moving. He hit the steps, rolled forward over his shoulders and with his feet, plucked the pistol from Nilsson's hand and dropped it over the railing.

And then the white man was on his feet, smiling, moving again toward Nilsson.

"Sorry," he said. "That's the biz, sweetheart."

Nilsson roared, deep down in his throat, a roar of generations of Viking raiders.

Perhaps, he thought. Perhaps the curse of Sinanju was on the Nilsson family. But he could still give meaning to Lhasa's death by fulfilling

179

the family contract. He turned from Remo and bolted up the stairs. The girl. He would rip her throat out.

He took the steps three at a time.

Remo turned on the landing and started up after him, but then stopped.

So did Nilsson. At the top of the stairs stood the ancient Oriental, serene and placid in his yellow robe, a smile on his face.

Remo could not hear his words, but it looked as if Chiun had said, "Welcome, Mr. Nilsson. Welcome to your famous house."

Nilsson thought to overpower him. Remo watched and smirked as he saw Nilsson's shoulders tense up for the charge he would make. Trying to charge Chiun was like trying to bite an alligator in the mouth. Nilsson roared again, lowered a shoulder and rammed forward against Chiun. The old man gave way, and Nilsson was past him. Remo shook his head in shock for a moment, then darted up the stairs after Nilsson.

Vickie stood behind Maggot and the band, watching them, tapping her foot. She turned and saw Nilsson racing toward her. Her eyes opened in fright as she registered the look on his face. She backed away.

Remo was at the top of the stairs now, but he saw only a flash of saffron robe moving across the stage. Nilsson's arms were extended in front of him, reaching for the girl.

The Viking roar rose again in his throat. It died in a curdled squeak as an iron-hard hand came from behind him. Nilsson's last thoughts were those of a physician, not an assassin. He recognized the crunch of temple bones breaking, the piercing pain as shards of bone sliced like

180

knives into his brain, and then the slow feeling of lazy warmth as death overtook his body.

He turned toward Chiun, searching those hazel eyes for meaning, but there was only respect. He turned again and staggered out onto the stage in front of Maggot and the Dead Meat Lice, who kept playing despite the intrusion. In his death throes, Nilsson weaved toward the edge of the stage, collapsed and rolled off, dropping the fifteen feet to the ground, landing on the shoulders of one of the guards who began to punch Nilsson's dead body, calling his friends to help him teach the troublemaker a lesson.

Up on the stage, Maggot shouted:

"Heavy, man. Dead Meat Lice rule over all."

Down below, the guards piled on Nilsson's helpless corpse. The cordon of protection between the bandstand and the audience disappeared.

It was a girl who made the first charge. One lone girl moving quickly across the grass toward the stage. Several others watched. When she was not stopped, a few more came, a trickle at first, then a wave, then a tsunami. Maggot stopped in the middle of a note. He saw the crowd rushing toward the platform and him. Hundreds of people. With unwashed hands. Greasy fingers. Dirty fingernails. Tobacco-stained knuckles. Trying to touch him. He hit the switch under his foot on the stage and smoke immediately began to pour up again from the machine underneath.

The music slowed and stopped. The sudden silence was like an invitation to charge. Baying like a pack of hounds, the entire audience seemed to surge forward toward the bandstand.

"Vickie, quick," Maggot yelled, he hit a second switch and under cover of the smoke, the lift in the center of the stage began to descend. The

181

Lice jumped onto the platform with Maggot. Remo put an arm around Vickie Stoner and helped her down onto the descending platform. Next to him, Remo saw Chiun.

A moment later, they were all in the helicopter and it was lifting away, just out of reach of hundreds of fans, who had engulfed the craft but had the sense to stay away from its whirling blades.

As if on cue, the helicopter rose, and heavy drops of rain began to fall, the fat heavy drops that typify mountain summer showers.

"You all right, Vickie?" Maggot was asking.

"Yes, Calvin," she said. Remo was surprised. Her voice was clear, strong, unmuffled, undrugged.

"What's with you?" Remo said. "Run out of pills?"

"No, straight man. I'm off that. I got a new high."

"What's that?"

"Calvin," she said, touching Maggot's arm. "We're getting married."

"Congratulations," Remo said. "Name the first one after me."

"We will, even though straight shit is a funny name for a boy baby."

Remo grinned. He looked out at the Darlington farm below. It had been raining only a few seconds but already the field was puddling and muddy in the cloudburst. People scurried back and forth, fights broke out all over the site. It looked like an aerial view of a Harlem riot. Anyone studying entropy, the principle of maximum confusion, would have recognized the field as a textbook illustration.

Remo felt Chiun's face next to his, peering out the chopper window.

"Tell me, Remo," Chiun said. "Is this a happening?"

"A what?"

"A happening."

"I guess it is," Remo said.

"Good," Chiun said. "I have always wanted to be at a happening."

The helicopter continued to circle the farm for a few minutes and then one of the Lice said to the pilot, "Better take it out of here, man, some of them cats may be packing heat."

The pilot tipped the nose forward and the craft swooshed off, back toward the town and the motel.

"I can't wait to get back," Vickie said.

"Why?" Remo said. "Anything special?"

"No. Just to call my daddy. Tell him I'm all right."

"Your father? You call him?"

"Every day. Just so he knows where I am and that I'm safe."

"This is the father you're going to testify against?"

"Yeah, but that's business. This other is personal, my calling him. I have to. He's just so depressed. Every time he hears my voice, he says, 'Oh, it's you,' like it's the end of the world."

"I understand," Remo said and for the first time, he did. He understood who had put out the contract on her life, and why there was so much money backing it up, and now he understood why the assassins always seemed to know exactly where Vickie Stoner was.

He understood a lot of things now.

He looked across the cabin at Chiun, who looked less queasy than he usually did when he was on a helicopter.

183

"You understand now, do you not?" Chiun asked.

"I do."

"In time, even a rock learns to be worn away by the water."

"Have you ever heard the sound of one hand clapping?" Remo asked.

CHAPTER TWENTY-ONE

Paul Stoner, Vickie's father, was easy.

He lived in a quarter-million dollar townhouse in New York's east Sixties, and his scream of death was just another on a block so used to screams that no one paid any attention to them anymore.

But before he died, he wrote a suicide note for Remo, implicating the other companies and financiers who had been involved in the Russian grain swindle which had driven the price of bread in America up by fifty percent.

Remo arranged the suicide to look like a suicide, then with the note in his hand, dialed Dr. Smith at the 800-area-code free-from-anywhere number.

"All over, Smitty," he said.

"Oh?"

"Yeah, Stoner's dead. He confessed everything in a suicide note. You want the note?"

"No. Leave it there. I'll make sure federal agents find the body. That way the note won't get lost."

"It says here in fine Japanese braille," Remo said sarcastically.

"Just leave the note," Smith said. "Anything else?"

"I guess Vickie won't have to testify now."

"No," Smith said. "Not with the note. That should cover everything."

He stopped and Remo waited, but neither spoke.

"Don't you think you owe Chiun an apology?" Remo finally asked.

"For what?"

"For not having any faith in his ability to handle the Nilssons?"

"Does he want the apology or do you?" Smith asked.

"Well, now that you mention it, I guess we both deserve it."

"When your paychecks aren't on time, then I'll apologize," Smith said.

"As ever, you're gracious to a fault. I hope your yogurt curdles," Remo said and hung up.

Later, back in their hotel room, he asked Chiun:

"One thing I don't understand, Little Father. When we saw him in the theater lobby, how'd you know that the old guy was Gunner Nilsson?"

"It is a strange thing about Swedish people," Chiun said.

"What is?" Remo asked.

"They all look alike."

Remo grunted. "At Darlington, how come he was able to put a shoulder into you?"

"I allowed him to."

"Why?" Remo asked.

"Because I promised his brother I would treat him with respect."

Remo searched Chiun's face. "Good for you," he said. "Toop, toop, toop."

"What is this toop, toop, toop?" Chiun asked.

"The sound of one hand clapping, of course."

THE EXECUTIONER
by Don Pendleton

Available wherever paperbacks are sold, or order direct from the Publisher. Send cover price plus 50¢ per copy for mailing and handling to Pinnacle Books, Dept. 17-195, 475 Park Avenue South, New York, N.Y. 10016. Residents of New York, New Jersey and Pennsylvania must include sales tax. DO NOT SEND CASH.

BLOCKBUSTER FICTION FROM PINNACLE BOOKS!

THE FINAL VOYAGE OF
THE S.S.N. SKATE   (17-157, $3.95)
by Stephen Cassell
The "leper" of the U.S. Pacific Fleet, SSN 578 nuclear attack sub SKATE, has one final mission to perform — an impossible act of piracy that will pit the underwater death-trap and its inexperienced crew against the combined might of the Soviet Navy's finest!

QUEENS GATE RECKONING   (17-164, $3.95)
by Lewis Purdue
Only a wounded CIA operative and a defecting Soviet ballerina stand in the way of a vast consortium of treason that speeds toward the hour of mankind's ultimate reckoning! From the best-selling author of THE LINZ TESTAMENT.

FAREWELL TO RUSSIA   (17-165, $4.50)
by Richard Hugo
A KGB agent must race against time to infiltrate the confines of U.S. nuclear technology after a terrifying accident threatens to unleash unmitigated devastation!

THE NICODEMUS CODE   (17-133, $3.95)
by Graham N. Smith and Donna Smith
A two-thousand-year-old parchment has been unearthed, unleashing a terrifying conspiracy unlike any the world has previously known, one that threatens the life of the Pope himself, and the ultimate destruction of Christianity!

Available wherever paperbacks are sold, or order direct from the Publisher. Send cover price plus 50¢ per copy for mailing and handling to Pinnacle Books, Dept. 17-195, 475 Park Avenue South, New York, N.Y. 10016. Residents of New York, New Jersey and Pennsylvania must include sales tax. DO NOT SEND CASH.